THE PLAGUES OF KONDAR

A NOVEL BY

LYNNE KOSITSKY

DUNDURN

TORONTO

Editor: Cheryl Hawley
Design: Jennifer Scott
Cover design by Courtney Horner.
Cover image: © traffic_analyzer/iStockphoto
Printer: Webcom

Library and Archives Canada Cataloguing in Publication

Kositsky, Lynne, 1947-, author
     The plagues of Kondar / Lynne Kositsky.

Issued in print and electronic formats.
ISBN 978-1-4597-0934-8 (pbk.).--ISBN 978-1-4597-0935-5 (pdf).--
ISBN 978-1-4597-0936-2 (epub)

     I. Title.

PS8571.O85P53 2014   jC813'.54   C2013-907397-3   C2013-907398-1

1 2 3 4 5   18 17 16 15 14

Conseil des Arts du Canada   Canada Council for the Arts   Canadä   ONTARIO ARTS COUNCIL
CONSEIL DES ARTS DE L'ONTARIO

We acknowledge the support of the **Canada Council for the Arts** and the **Ontario Arts Council** for our publishing program. We also acknowledge the financial support of the **Government of Canada** through the **Canada Book Fund** and **Livres Canada Books**, and the **Government of Ontario** through the **Ontario Book Publishing Tax Credit** and the **Ontario Media Development Corporation**.

Visit us at
Dundurn.com | @dundurnpress | Facebook.com/dundurnpress |
Pinterest.com/Dundurnpress

Dundurn	Gazelle Book Services Limited	Dundurn
3 Church Street, Suite 500	White Cross Mills	2250 Military Road
Toronto, Ontario, Canada	High Town, Lancaster, England	Tonawanda, NY
M5E 1M2	LA1 4XS	U.S.A. 14150

In loving memory of my friend and doctor,
Robert Buckman, who cheered me up when I was down
and told me not to sell the furniture.

CHAPTER ONE

There have long been tales of ghosts and ghouls inhabiting Oscura, the dark side of Kondar. "An old, old man I met today, while clearing snow from our pathway," my father says, "too ancient even to be a seer, swore that there are creatures living on Oscura who many cycles ago flew across Edge onto Lightside. He says he saw and heard them as they writhed and screamed before they evaporated in a swirl of mist. Many of the dwellers who watched grew sick and died."

"Hush," Mother responds, as she scrubs the table clean. "Not in front of the child."

"I'm not a child!" I protest sharply. Her words irritate me. "I'm fifteen cycles. Almost."

"No one sane believes him anyway. His mind is addled with age," Father continues, ignoring my mother and me, "and his teeth are rotted out. He must be a baseborn."

Mother purses her lips and works harder, as she always does when listening to or speaking of unsettling incidents.

And there are always plenty of them to speak of. Father says that we live on a malevolent, dangerous planet, as if there were other planets close by. "Could there be other planets that exist? Planets safer than ours?" I ask, but he's lost interest in the conversation and is gazing into space. Brain travelling, I call it. Much to Mother's disgust, Father does a lot of brain travelling.

Mother makes small disapproving snorts before taking out her sewing. She is stitching together squares for a quilt. Drawing the needle in and out of the material too fast, she pricks her finger and a bead of orange blood appears. She wipes her hand on her apron, so she doesn't get it on the quilt. It leaves a spreading orangey-brown smear. Her blood, the same colour as mine, tells of our ancestry, the ancient house we're descended from. It reminds us not to spill it unnecessarily.

"The old man's ridiculous. He'd probably been drinking too much gulrid ale and imagined or nightmared the whole thing. How can anyone survive in Oscura? It's far too dark and cold as a grave." I don't want to entertain the possibility that as well as a frozen wasteland unvisited by the sun, there might be horrible winged creatures beyond Edge. It's too frightening.

"The ways of the gods are strange indeed." Mother folds up the fabric she's been sewing. "And their miracles are never ending. Who knows who or what might be on the other side of Edge, good or bad? But as long as we're over here, we don't have to think about it." She puts the unfinished quilt away on a shelf and starts sweeping.

"But Mother ..."

"Hush, Arien, don't question, and never venture too close to Edge or you might be pulled across."

"There's a happy thought. Who by?"

"Never mind, daughter. That's enough discussion for today." She has begun to alarm herself with her talk and shivers slightly. Leaning her broom against the table she raises both palms to her forehead, making her prayer sign. Her palms leave two whitish marks on her temples. This is the signal for me to go silent, else I'll be banished to my room. During the absence of conversation, I think of what she's said. Lightside has evils enough. Why would I ever go near Edge?

Mother has always been nervous that something untoward could happen to me. So nervous, in fact, that she often stops me from saying what I want to say — arresting me in mid-sentence — or doing what I want to do. Although she can't stop me thinking what I want to think, I sometimes feel as if I'm trapped inside the small box of what she allows; a prisoner to her will. But I'm her only child, and although she keenly desires to she can't have another, so there are no other sons or daughters on whom she can bestow her anxiety. All of it is focused on me. She continually worries about my safety, while finding extended discussions involving perils and accidents disturbing. She has her own way of ending an argument concerning what I may or may not do or what is or is not dangerous to my wellbeing. It usually involves multiple prayers, a basketful of dire predictions, and a widening chasm of silence between us.

I want to talk more. I want to be reassured. The terrors of Edge have been drummed into me for so long that I am almost as horrified by it as she is. Edge is sinister, separating Lightside — where we live and where the sun shines its face upon us — from Oscura, which is shut up in eternal night. Occasionally I see flashes of orange-white lightning emanating from it, though we're too far away to hear the accompanying thunder. When the day is clear, in cold Icer or hot Solar, I can see its foggy grey wall in the distance, high as a mountain, where light and dark clash and entwine. It shuts out sun. It casts a pall. It leads to Oscura — the unknown — a world possibly inhabited by creatures more frightening than death dragons.

After what Father has said about the old man with rotted teeth, when I enter the cloudy doors of sleep I dream of taloned monsters dragging me from light into blackness. I shriek, but no one comes. There is no one left alive *to* come. Another recurring nightmare: looking out the window of my room I see hideous creatures diving to the ground below, then stretching their arms up, up, up, till they lengthen enough to grab me. The dream always ends there, though it's usually conflated with another dream about a feast of roast grunt meat, which I scarf down greedily until my belly is full and I'm merry. So I have no idea what happens after I'm grabbed. I'm sure I wouldn't want to.

I've only experienced real dark once, when I was about five cycles old; I shut myself in the clothing chest by mistake when playing hide-and-find with my friend Radol. The clasp was on the outside. My terror began when I heard it click shut, trapping me. The blackness and smell of unwashed clothes were suffocating. I screamed over and over before fainting. When I came to I discovered that Radol had unlocked the chest and flung its lid wide open before reporting the calamity to Mother. She had smacked him and sent him home. She had a strong hand. I'd often felt it. It left deep purple imprints on my skin.

"But I didn't do anything," Radol howled. He rubbed his backside as he ran out the door.

She was now leaning over me, her eyes pools of concern. But if I was expecting her to utter a few words of sympathy, I was disappointed. "What have I told you about climbing into that chest?" she snapped. "You bad, bad girl. I should slap you too. Don't ever do it again."

I've never hidden under the bed, in a chest, or any other enclosed space since; I've never deliberately gone where dark might jump out and seize me. I won't do it in a game or for a dare. I've totally avoided it. The closest I've ever come to darkness, apart from when I close my eyes — though I mostly see shifting patterns of brilliant triangles, squares, and circles rather than blackness when I do — is the twilight shadow of nights during Icer, or opaque banks of blackish-red cloud ready to burst rain or sleet into the wind. As opaque shadows descend on me as these clouds pass overhead, they feel like the cobwebs that crawlers weave, sticky and macabre.

The snow isn't deep today. There's even been a little run-off. But when Icer days are drifted with snow almost to the rooftops, shutting out the sun, there is again that ghastly eeriness. Outside sounds are as muted as they were in the clothing chest, and I feel as faint now as I did then. I'm a fainter by nature, forever falling into a heap or passing out completely. I'm the bane, Mother tells me, of her existence. She says I need to toughen up. But she says it kindly.

Leader taught us last Solar that Kondar has two moons. "They are there in case the sun fails," he said confidently. "Like beacons in the sky. It is the gods' way of taking care of us."

"I want to see them," I tell Father.

"The moons or the gods?" Father asks. He sounds absent, somewhere else entirely. He's brain travelling again.

"The moons, of course. But Leader said they only really reveal themselves in darkness. All I've glimpsed is an occasional ghostly outline in a pink evening sky. Come to think of it, how does Leader know that there isn't just one moon, or five or six?"

Father doesn't look up. He's writing runes on scraps of wood; the prepared surface of the wood is small, and the runes themselves so difficult to form in the available space that his fingers constantly cramp. He puts down his stylus and raises his hands every so often, clenching and unclenching them to banish stiffness before rubbing them together. He clearly has no desire to get into a lengthy discussion about the unprovable moons of Kondar, but I persist.

"There are also three other planets in our system, according to Leader. He says there might be dwellers on them. One planet is bigger, two smaller than Kondar. I haven't seen them either. As a matter of fact, has he seen them? How could he? But otherwise, how would he know?"

Father sighs. "Maybe the seers told him. I've heard it mentioned myself."

"How would the seers know?" I persisted.

"Their knowledge comes from the mythical stories of long ago. I've told you before that in ancient times, each day was divided into two: a period of light and another of darkness. They saw the moons and stars in the dark period. I can't imagine what it would be like."

"Me neither. I don't think I could stand being in the dark for half of every day. But it probably didn't happen. As I get older, I'm starting to have a problem believing in things I can't see."

Father at last looks up. He appears troubled. "What about the gods?"

"Well, the gods are different, of course," I say quickly, afraid to displease him. "I don't have to see them to know they're there." But sometimes in quiet moments I wonder if they really *are* there. I pray for all sorts of things — more food, sugar-fruit, or even an extra quilt in Icer — but no one answers and nothing changes. I would never voice my qualms aloud though. Mother says that one non-believer might anger the gods so much they could destroy our entire settlement of Katannya. And I certainly wouldn't want to be responsible for that. Not that I am a non-believer. But I can't help having doubts. So I change the subject. "And Leader says there used to be another season, Atam. He says the oldest dwellers in Katannya still talk of it."

"It's true. There must have been a wobble," says Father, "in Kondar's orbit."

I give him a sharp look, not sure whether he's joking. His face is turned away so I can't tell. But whatever the reason, weather often shifts from scorching to freezing overnight, as Solar smashes headlong into Icer. I can feel the jolt. My bones crack like an old man's knuckles. At first, as I wake to cool sheets in a cold room, I feel immediate relief, tuck my hands beneath the quilt and curl my toes up in its warmth. But soon our dwelling is beset by vicious gales that howl around our settlement, blowing shutters off window frames and branches off skytrees. Sometimes a roof thatched with dried ducan grass, or indeed a whole dwelling, blows away. I've seen enough debris fly past my window to build a new home. When I hear the terrible and insistent clamour of the wind, making the timbers of our dwelling shift and moan, I huddle fearfully in my bed and try to rock myself to sleep. But no amount of wishing or praying helps as the god of Icer — so it is said — vents his rage on our settlement.

At such times, we wrap ourselves in quilts or the skins of drogs or burden beasts, and many in the poorer dwellings huddle together for warmth. Some dwellers still die during the frigid weather, though several cycles ago fire was brought by torch from another settlement further north, together with instructions for creating it. It was presented to Chief Seer as a gift. Our seers then asked the gods, in one of their mysterious council meetings, for permission to use this new sun-like heat, and the gods apparently answered in a satis-factory way. It sounded a bit suspicious to me. Why would the gods be interested in whether we used fire or not? The seers, on the other hand, might well be if the outcome was to their advantage. "The gods decree that flames of fire should be allowed in dwellings," intoned Chief Seer, after gathering us dwellers about him. He was the first to build fires in his own home, making a hole in his roof for smoke to escape.

No one in our settlement had ever seen fire in a dwelling before, or heard the crackling of flames in a hearth, though we'd all seen forests burn. The adults had previously thought fire too perilous to enclose, and Mother was always warning me to heed its dangers. But the flames were said by the seers to be magical. After visiting Chief Seer's large dwelling and discussing the matter, my parents agreed that fire certainly warmed up his home. And after he told them that many of the other settlements had tamed fire for years for use in their homes, my parents quickly followed his example. In the old days we had to heat a stone in a hot spring — there are several springs in Katannya that boil and bubble in both Solar and Icer — then drop it into a cook pot to heat soup or stew. It was heavy work carrying the stones back and forth, and Mother's fingers often got singed. I would watch her as she applied flutterer fat to her burns. "Stay away from the hot stones," she would admonish me, "or they'll take the skin off you."

Now we can cook over fire in our home. Mother hooks the pot over a long metal arm and stirs it constantly. When I'm outside, I often see the smoke from the blaze billowing over roofs. It curls itself into cloud-like pictures and rises even higher before dissipating. I love the ashy end-of-cycle smell of it; it's how I imagine Atam must have smelled.

Yet even the magic flames are no match for freezing temperatures. The wind still howls; snow and sleet still enter through cracks in our walls, melting to small puddles on the floor. When storms roar, rattling the doors and windows, I sometimes lie upstairs for days, wrapped in my quilt, all my clothes piled on top of me for extra warmth. Father often pushes a small hatch in the roof open and builds a fire in the stone hearth of my room, but even that's not entirely satisfactory; as smoke drifts up through the hole, snow blows down it. And Mother feels that one fire in the house is quite enough to worry about. She doesn't, she says, need to have nightmares about two.

"Get out of bed and do something useful," she scolds. I don't want to. There's no school during Icer. The students, especially the littler ones, would be blown away trying to get there. Leader gives us plenty of homework instead. It consists mainly of committing to memory — or trying to

— what he said last Solar. I sometimes wonder whether he can read and write. He seems to have no inkling of whether a rune is right-side up. When he sees me writing, he neglects to comment. Perhaps he can't see whether what I'm doing is right or wrong.

In any case, there's little to get up for except the occasional bowl of vegetable soup or a minute slice of salt meat that grows ever smaller as Icer progresses. But one afternoon the wind blows so hard and lightning strikes so close by that I fear a skytree might crash into our dwelling, knocking it down with all of us inside. I can already hear skytrees scraping against our windowpane, as if their branches are beset by the bone ague. Pushing myself out of bed, I tiptoe over to the window, only to see twigs and branches flying by, accompanied by heavy swathes of snow. A bough hits my window so hard it cracks the glass. Shocked, I rush downstairs to be near my parents. I feel safer downstairs.

"I'm scared," I admit to Father.

"It's a terrible storm," he agrees. He holds me to him until the worst of it passes. "Want to play hide-and-find?"

Father's idea of hide-and-find is to sit at the table while I discover a place to stow away upstairs before he calls out, "Are you in the loft? Are you in your room? Are you hiding under your bed?" When he guesses right the game is over and he goes back to his runes.

"Thank you, but I've decided I'm too old to play that game. It's boring. And in any case, I came *downstairs* to avoid being *upstairs*."

"It's no secret that the weather is worsening." Mother is back to the subject of storms. "Some of the seers gathered together the more important dwellers recently and told them that at least one god, the god of Icer, is not pleased at the discovery of fire. They say that because of it, he blows his savage winter blasts at us all with a new ferocity. I know because I was at the meeting." She frowns. "The Chief Seer is keeping his fire burning, but perhaps we should extinguish ours."

"Icer, as I've said many times before, is encroaching a little more every cycle. So is dark. Nevertheless, we should keep the fire burning, as perhaps one day Icer will knock out the other seasons altogether. Then there'll only be snow," Father says as he sharpens his stylus.

"Now there's a pleasant thought. How would we grow our crops if that happened?" Mother asks.

"I dare say we wouldn't be able to."

Mother grimaces. She's stirring the broth, watery though it is, as there's not so much as a broken grunt bone left to put in it. But not even an Icer storm stops her working. In fact, it tends to do the opposite. When she's busy she can't imagine all the horrible things that could happen, or so she tells me. Meanwhile she tends the flames as though they might reach out and bite her. Fire is high on her list when it comes to tales of disastrous accidents. It's right up there with Edge.

"Careful," Mother warns, as I place the log under the pot. "Desperate as a caged thief is fire. It sometimes escapes its rightful place and roars through dwellings, licking along walls and roofs, burning through wood and ducan, making a conflagration of the homes, sometimes with entire families trapped inside."

I sigh. Though I know she speaks out of love, a wish to protect me, fire is my best friend during freezing weather.

"Not in front of the child, Danara," says Father, mocking what Mother constantly says. She glares at him before making the prayer sign.

Oh, we are a happy crew, I think, as I sit down at table and take up my spoon. "Happy, happy Icer."

CHAPTER TWO

I feel a slight lessening of cold, like the loosening of a tunic belt, when I go outside, so I begin to feel hopeful. Farlis, the brief season between Icer and Solar, must be close. I report this sign of better times to Mother. Perhaps she'll bury her fears of death by fire for the time being. She smiles, erasing some of the lines on her face. It is a blessing to get a smile out of her. She seldom smiles.

There is a lightness to the air, and the flutterers are chirping. One has already built a nest by the front door and is sitting in it. I can almost smell the heady scent of hedge roses, though the buds aren't visible yet. But as usual, my thoughts soon return to food. I've lost weight over Icer. My clothes hang on me like empty grain sacks. When I look at my reflection in the glass I see a face that is thin and scrawny, with dark shadows under the eyes and in the hollows of the cheeks. It's no wonder. I have a continual and painful rumbling in my belly from lack of nourishment. Mother's soup yesterday was so thin it was little more than heated snow water. My stomach gurgled as I spooned it down and that was an end to it. I'm still starving.

As if in answer to my belly grumbling, Mother says, as I enter the dwelling, "Your father and I are going across Icer Lake to see whether the settlement of Gloyn has more grain than we do and can spare some. Why, there isn't even seed left to plant. I was sure we harvested enough and more to tide us over Icer, but it's all gone."

"Let me come with you," I beg, fearful of being left alone. "Suppose another storm comes along and knocks our dwelling down with me inside it?"

Mother doesn't reply; she scrubs the table so hard that dirty water sloshes onto the floor.

"Won't happen now. Too late in the season." Father begins to sing softly to himself. His arms wave in the air like skytree branches, but not because his fingers are cramping. He's conducting. Who or what, I have no idea.

"We just *had* a storm," I point out.

"It was the last one of the season," he replies with confidence. There's no use asking him how he knows. He'll just say that the skytrees whisper it to him. Strange though it is, the skytrees are often correct. Their songs and murmurs have become our family's weathercock. Occasionally, even I hear the dreamy sounds of their music when I sit under their branches.

"You stay here, Arien," says Mother, as she mops the floorboards. "You're a young woman now, as you're always telling me, old enough, surely, to look after yourself for a few days. There's Blanta next door you can call on if anything worrying happens. Besides, if we take you with, there won't be room for grain on the sledge during the return trekken. And the way can be dangerous. I wouldn't want you to overbalance onto the ice. You could get a nasty bruise. Or you might go through it." She tucks a stray lock of hair behind her ear with a trembling hand.

"Please, Mother. I'm not afraid of danger when I'm with you."

"Perhaps not, but I am. You're not coming, and that's that. It's safer here. But don't go out of the dwelling unless it's over to Blanta's. And don't let strangers in." Mother shakes her head three times. I know from experience that one shake means that she can be persuaded if I pester her long enough, two means it's not likely that anything will change, and three means there's no hope of her relenting, not even if the dwelling is on fire and the sky falls down on top of it. My parents leave on the sledge soon after, drawn by a burden beast borrowed from Blanta.

"Go on then, take him." Blanta had been scraping the path clear of snow when Mother and I walked across to ask. "The beast needs the exercise; he's been shut in the barn all Icer. Wrap his feet so they don't freeze."

"Of course," replied Mother.

Now Mother and Father have been gone for some time. I imagine they will lead the burden beast and carry the sledge on their shoulders as they come quickly back by land. The ice would be too thin now, and they're experts at testing it. They'll be here soon. The sledge is light and their feet are still swift, I tell myself. For a moment I forget the heavy bags of grain they might be bringing with them, but soon I remember. Where would they put it if they're carrying the sledge? They could be significantly slowed if they try to haul sledge and grain over the rocks and pebbles surrounding the lake if they have to go around rather than across.

Three days ago, when they left, all was snow and frost. Two days later rain pelted down, thrumming its hard rhythms onto the roof all night. It left muddy puddles on the path in its wake. Today is sun and the water is retreating. After laying trenchers on the table in preparation for my parents' return — although goodness knows there won't be much to eat unless they've been fortunate at the Gloyn settlement — I stand by the open door and watch with pleasure yellow clouds scudding across purple sky and ducan pushing through earth and almost melted snow. Violent winds, their whistling like the noisy breathing of old women, grow lazy and vanish, leaving only a wafting breeze behind them, redolent with the scent of buds and blossoms. The crouched skytrees of Icer unfurl and rise to their full height, roots climbing red and green trunks, branches untwisting, blue leaves unfolding.

My pleasure is tinged with a shadowy sadness. I've always wanted freedom. Now I have it, but instead of rejoicing I feel my aloneness keenly. I've never been left by myself for so long, and my isolation is as sharp as a knife. I'm sure Mother must be as worried about me as I am about her and Father. But the boughs are singing quiet skytree songs, the kind Father loves, and they remind me of him. When home, Father writes their words down using his special tree runes, so he can sing them during celebrations. No one else sings like Father. The words sound mystical and otherworldly. At first I couldn't hear the skytrees singing, but Father told me to listen carefully. After a great deal of concentration, I began to hear them in my head, as he does. Now I hear them all the time. Sometimes now, I can even hear what the flutterers and flowers are saying, though much of the time they just babble, as their brains are so small, their thoughts so silly. Often I wonder whether I'm imagining things.

I can't wait for him — and Mother too, of course — to come back, dragging the sledge through half-melted snow. I offer a prayer for their safety. It's easy enough to believe in the gods when I need something from them.

Farlis is far too short lately, sometimes shifting into Solar after only a few days, but I mean to enjoy every minute of it as soon as my parents return. I take a shallow breath as hope is once again replaced by fear for their wellbeing. It's selfish, but I can't help thinking that my own safety depends on theirs; however, the cold that pinched my nose all Icer so my nostrils stuck together and I couldn't breathe properly has gone. And that's a good sign.

I am waiting, waiting, waiting impatiently. I peer through the door again, but no one is on the horizon. One skytree, though, is so energized by the mild weather that it's dancing in the slush, its branches swaying to its own rhythm. I could swear it's moving closer to the dwelling on little wooden toes. But every time I look at it, it stops. I listen very hard so I can hear those rhythms myself. I sway too, twirl until I'm so dizzy I bump into a chair. I'm not a very good dancer at the best of times, but that doesn't stop me galloping around like a fool when I'm happy or sad. Now I'm both, though mainly happy, because as well as my parents, my old friend Radol should be coming soon. I love Radol dearly, although I'm never allowed to say so.

"It's too early," Mother protested when I once mentioned Radol and love in the same breath. "You're a child. He's not much older. You might care for him, but you don't know what love is. You can't betroth until your seventeenth cycle anyway." I find it galling that I'm considered a grown-up when she needs me to be and a child when she doesn't. At that moment I was a child because she didn't want to lose me to the far-off settlement where Radol lives. "Radol's a nice boy," she went on, "clean, neat, and polite, but you'll probably outgrow him in a cycle or two."

"Never," I replied. "We've been friends since we were babies." We grew up together, even though he was a whole cycle older than I. We spent frozen seasons playing in each other's dwellings, and he saved me from the horrors of the wooden chest. When the cold evaporated each cycle, in Farlis and early Solar, we trekkened along the trails that ringed our settlement. "I can't imagine ever outgrowing him."

"That's enough," said Mother, making her prayer sign and drawing her brows together as if a storm were threatening. And in a way it was. Mother can have a nasty temper when crossed, or simply harry me half to death when she wants compliance. So all I say in front of her now is that I like him, which is a pallid term indeed.

"Come quickly, Radol," I shout into the empty room. "I'll never love anyone else." I wouldn't say this in front of my parents, or to Radol himself for that matter. But when alone I can say whatever I like. There are some advantages, after all, in having the dwelling to myself. But it would be far better to have him close by.

"Little cousin," he has always called me. "Little cousin, come collect nuts and berries with me along the path. Only the safe berries, mind. I'll show you those you must never touch." Or, "Little cousin, come down to Dead Pool and swim. It's safe there. Nothing either good or evil exists in it." He always looked after me in this way, especially when I was very young, though we weren't real cousins. Even so, we were inseparable as twins, though we look nothing like each other — he's tall and fair, I'm short and dark like my mother. But I haven't seen him since the first snows fell, as two cycles ago he moved to another settlement, Ongis, nearer to the central area of Lightside.

He now lives with his family in the region of the smoke mountains — mountains that belch steam and fire when provoked. Radol told me this the last time he was in Katannya as well as describing the Cauldron to me. Apparently it's the remains of an old "smokie," as he taught me to call smoke mountains, lying under a deep orange lake, as uninhabited as Dead Pool; jagged black cliffs surround it. In my imagination the lake is silent, smooth as a mirror. I stare into it. It reflects my face. Wavelets lap the corners of my brain. The people of Ongis believe a god lives inside the Cauldron and pray that he will keep them safe if it erupts. Radol thinks the smokie collapsed after exploding many cycles ago. Flat though it is, it can unleash its flash and fury at any time; he says it sounds like thunder as it emits steam from inside its crater, which sticks up like a small island in the lake. So it's not like the quiet Cauldron of my mind at all. I can't imagine what might provoke smokies or their gods, if gods there are, but just the *possibility* of their anger alarms me.

In spite of the smokies that belch and spit — flat as lake floors or incredibly lofty, pointing like sawn-off fingers towards the sky — the family moved to Ongis because the weather is milder there and Icer tends to end earlier so that the grain and fruit harvest is richer. They were ready to take the risk. But suppose, in its rage, the God of the *Cauldron* destroys Radol's settlement?

"I promise to visit each Farlis, after crops are planted and there is nothing much for me to do until the end of Solar except sit on the ground and watch them grow," he said as they packed up to leave. "I can't visit when ice is treacherous enough to be impassable, or snow piles so high it hides the skytrees. It would be too dangerous to trekken. But I wish I could be here with you."

"I would like that," I replied shyly.

"When we're adults we can be together for always. But for now, come our Farlis, I will rake and plant as fast as I can, and then I will be with you as yours begins."

Be together for always? I can't imagine anything more wonderful! Last cycle he showed that he meant to keep his promise about returning. He appeared on the fourth day of Farlis, hair shining, grin crooked, gait loping. He'd grown at least two thumbs higher and I barely reached his shoulders. Perhaps this cycle he's even taller. But I really shouldn't expect him yet. I could be dreadfully disappointed. Today is only the third warm day in Katannya. He might not come until tomorrow or even later if the planting has taken longer than usual.

After snow melted in the past, when he lived nearby, I felt that Icer had never existed, that I'd dreamed the snow piled at the door as well as the lace on frost's window. But the first Icer without Radol was nightmarish and seemed to go on forever. I worried whether the Cauldron had blasted apart once more, its lava streams killing everything before them in their rush to break free of the frigid underworld of the lake. And when the snow finally cleared, I was haunted by the memory of Radol until I saw him again and was sure he'd survived. But this cycle I am more certain that Farlis will bring him back to me — like a glittering stone returned by waves to the shore — for he told me after I confessed my fears that if the Cauldron ever erupted, we would feel it right here in Katannya. It would shake the ground violently, and there's been no ground-shaking at all, so my mind is almost completely at ease.

Radol is so clever to know all that he knows. Cleverer than Leader. And he's kind besides. Perhaps he will bring a gift for me, a dried lush-fruit or nectar-peach. Such delicacies don't grow in Katannya. Our climate doesn't support them. Most important, though, he will bring himself, untouched by smokie fire, call me his little cousin again.

Late in the evening he still hasn't arrived; neither have my parents. I can hardly bear the thought of another night alone. I'm always most afraid at bedtime. Although it is still as light as midday, the flutterers and skytrees cease their songs, and there is a blackness in my mind that no amount of sunshine can dispel. Every creak and groan either inside or out — sounds that I never notice when my parents are home — echo like wraithy footsteps through the dwelling. I imagine thieves, monsters, ghosts outside my door, waiting to snare me when I crack it open.

Suddenly I hear my mother. "*Arien, Arien,*" she cries. "*Come quickly.*" With whoops of joy I rush downstairs to lift the latch, but she isn't outside. My brain has deceived me: I've conjured her up.

CHAPTER THREE

I'm unable to sleep. I toss restlessly for hours, throwing off the quilt and looking for a cool place on the pillow. Finally I get up and sit on a ledge in the loft, my legs slung over a window frame, feet dangling. I haven't put my luggers on, so I can wiggle my toes. They get tired of being squashed into heavy leather all Icer, so I go barefoot the rest of the cycle whenever I can, sweaty footwear thrown into a corner until the next Icer dictates another outing for them. I've had this pair for at least three cycles. I don't seem to grow much. Neither do my feet, though they must have gotten a bit bigger, as when I put them on, my big toes scrape against the front of the luggers. They also leave painful sores on my heels.

The loft is across from my room. From it I can see more easily if someone approaches. The single window faces south. That's the direction both Radol and my parents will come from, over our southern hill, though there's no sign of any of them at present.

I feel calmer this morning. The awful nervousness in the pit of my stomach has vanished. My anxiety has been replaced by dreaminess. The loft is beginning to smell of warm weather, of apple-fruits and dried ducan, though nothing remains of them except the musty scent and a few blades of ancient grass. I sniff appreciatively, thinking of the harvest to come. The smell reminds me that I'm starving, so I go downstairs to stoke the fire and boil the last bit of grain. There is so little of it that there is almost nothing to mash. I'll eat it straight out of the pot.

As I sit down I hear someone call from outside. "Arien, Arien, come quickly." This time it *must* be Mother, returned with Father at last. I put my spoon down and rush out. I'm dying to see her, promise myself that I'll never get upset at her nagging again. But I'm disappointed. It's not Mother. It's only bleary-eyed Blanta, probably come to check on me or say that she needs the burden beast back. She's the last person I want to see, but I notice immediately that something isn't right. She looks strange, angry, her face contorted. After trying to speak several times, her mouth stopped by invisible glue, making me wonder what I could possibly have done wrong, Blanta finds her voice and screams: "Your parents are dead."

"What?"

"You heard me. They went through the ice. And my burden beast went with them. How can I manage without him?"

"No they didn't. I don't believe you. You lie." This must be a horrid joke. There's a crushing pain in my heart and I can't breathe. It cannot — simply cannot — be true. My parents are just beyond the hill. They're climbing up it. When they reach its crest I'll see their faces and run to them. They'll be here within the hour.

They're too experienced with the sledge not to go around the lake if the ice is thinning. They can't have fallen in. They'll be here soon, I tell myself again. Even if they did happen to fall in, they're good swimmers. They'd never stay under. They'd never leave me. Nothing can keep them from coming home. In the middle of my desperate but silent denials I realize a young man is standing beside Blanta. I don't know him, have never seen him before. His face is dirty and his long hair oily. And despite the starvation that we have in Katannya, he is fat as a grunt. He must come from further south. I drag in a mouthful of air, whoosh it back out.

Blanta gestures to him. "My nephew Farun saw it all. Oh, evil, evil day. How shall I bring in crops without my poor old beast?"

"I did indeed see it," he says smoothly. "I was on my way here to visit Aunt Blanta when it happened. I crawled across the frozen lake and dived into the hole where the ice had given way. I tried to save them, but they had sunk to the bottom, weighted down as they were by burden beast and grain. I dived again and again, but the waterweed had tied knots around them. I did what I could and stayed down there as long as possible, but I had to scramble out before it got me too." He shakes his head, twisting his face into a grimace of concern.

I don't know how to answer him, but I feel both frantic and faint, taste blood because I've bitten my tongue. Rage bubbles up in me. I want to kick Blanta's stupid nephew over and over again for bringing such false but calamitous news, and for sounding so *rehearsed*. I want to kick Blanta too, for caring more about the burden beast than my parents.

I feel a sudden shock of realization. They're dead. Mother's voice — if it *was* Mother's voice — was calling me frantically from Icer Lake. The knowledge hits me like a hammer blow. In my imagination my parents turn and twist in the freezing water as if dancing, trying to fight off the weed, but it binds them fast, strong as the thickest rope. They cannot get free of it. They are at the bottom of the lake, their dance for life soon over, their bodies mangled. They will never, ever, come back. I am alone. I'm too shocked to sob. I turn as cold as they must have been at the end, my heart encased in ice.

"The sad thing is," the nephew goes on blandly, as if not sad at all, "yesterday, just two days later, Farlis arrived and they would have known to go around rather than over, although it would have taken them much longer."

I still don't speak. I know they were trying to get home fast because Mother, as usual, was concerned about me. Even when doing fieldwork she comes back at intervals to check on me, or to make sure I've arrived home from school safely. But even so, they knew about lake conditions better than anyone. How could they not realize that the ice was melting? Their death is a horrible mystery, but even worse, it is tainted by a nasty, slimy thought: *If Mother had let me go with, I would be dead now too.*

I go back into the dwelling, vacillating between belief and disbelief. I lie on my bed, cover myself with my quilt, kick it off, rise again, stand on one foot like a long-legged wading flutterer, sob, shriek, pace back and forth. I examine every corner of the dwelling, go in and out of every room over and over again, still half expecting to see my parents, Mother making up small packages of grain for the other dwellers, Father writing skytree songs and skipping around the cookroom with me when not brain travelling. I keep looking for them, continually rinsing my hands in a basin as if I'm guilty, as if I've committed an unspeakable act and need to cleanse myself. I can't sleep. And why would I be able to? What's happened is unimaginable. Their deaths have created a huge rip in the fabric of my life. It can't be mended.

Radol arrives while I'm pacing. When he hears what happened, he makes me sit at the table and sits down next to me. My legs swing up and down as if I'm still walking. My hand covers my mouth to stop me screaming. He tries his best to comfort me. It isn't until days later — when he's no longer with me — I understand he needed comforting himself. He was closer to Danara and Kaden — he called them by their given names — than to his own parents. But when he comes in, gift in hand, I barely notice him. I'm still too beset with rage and sadness. I can only say, over and over: "Father promised to teach me how to write down skytree songs. Now it is too late."

"Skytrees sing?" he asks softly.

"They sing into my mind … and Father's." I choke back a sob and manage to quiet my legs by pushing both hands into them. "But what can it matter now?"

He puts his arm around me. After many hours I realize that he hasn't called me "little cousin." Not once. He knew as soon as he saw me what I did not, that grief had grown me up.

CHAPTER FOUR

"You have to eat, Arien. You haven't grown an inch since last cycle and you're thin as a stick. Where are your stores?" Radol searches the dwelling but finds nothing. The small set of shelves near the hearth is entirely bare.

I'm recalling the story that the old beggar man told Father, of Oscurans falling into Lightside and writhing and screaming before they died. Could it really have happened? If so, they must have been in agony. I compare their fate to that of my parents. Is coming through Edge the same as crashing through ice? Did my parents suffer as horribly as the creatures of darkness? Was the story of the Darksiders' fate a bad omen that I should have recognized? If I had, I could have forewarned my parents and they might still be alive.

"Stores?" I answer Radol at last, dragging my mind back to the present. My voice sounds hollow, remote, as if I'm dredging up words from the bottom of Icer Lake.

"Of grain."

"We have no grain. It's all gone." When I say *we* I mean my family, but there is no *we* now, not unless I'm speaking of Radol and myself. Exhausted by grief and lack of sleep, I fold my arms on the table and put my head down, like when I was a little girl during my first days at school.

I haven't slept in two days. Last night the sun shone brightly, and a strong beam, hitting the window at an acute angle, felt as though it was piercing my eyelids and spearing right through me. I turned over, but it made little difference. I could still see my parents in the sunbeam's sharp shine. They were flying through air; they were falling through ice; they were going down, down, into the frost-sullen depths, where the savage water weed, hunting for prey in its ghastly underworld, discovered them. It wrapped its ropey chains around their bodies and squeezed hard, choking all life out of them. Mother was calling to me as she died. I'm sure of it. I shuddered when I was told about her death, and I shudder again now. As a small child I was cautioned by Mother to stay clear of Icer Lake. I know only too well that there's nothing left of my parents. What the waterweed didn't take care of, the grinders and spikelfish did.

"Vegetables? Fruit?" asks Radol.

"No. Neither, except what you brought. How can you think of eating at such a time?" I sit up, my voice clotted with anger. "Have the lush fruit if you want it." It lies on the table, dried up, wrinkled, his gift to me. I roll it across the table to him, can't bear to put it in my own mouth, or imagine the taste of it. My stomach churns. The idea of food, of chewing then swallowing it, sickens me.

"You must eat or you'll die. Your parents are gone, and

there's nothing either of us can do about it, but I'm not prepared to lose you too." He pauses, eyes red with tears.

"I can't eat. My belly is filled with grief."

"You have to. We could ask your neighbour if she has something," he says at last, slowly, as if afraid of the response, as well he might be.

"Old Blanta? With her fat, conceited nephew who I bet never went near the lake that day, never mind into it?"

"Someone else in the settlement, then." Radol sounds exhausted. Perhaps he is rethinking his affection for me. I wouldn't blame him, but I can't stop my despair and fury at the hand Fortune has dealt my family. As Radol's the only person present, he's the unfortunate victim of my ire.

"We're all starving. Icer was worse than ever. No one will have anything to spare except the seers, who tithed our crops last year, and they're not sharing." I feel a spiteful sense of victory, though there's nothing whatever to feel victorious about.

"Then I'll return and fetch grain from my family. We suffered no shortages during Icer. I can be there and back in two or at most three days." His voice remains quiet, sad.

"I want ..."

"And don't ask if you can come. I need to travel fast, so alone is best." He's probably eager to leave after the way I've treated him. I immediately feel sorry for my disgraceful behaviour but am too proud to say so. I remonstrate with him instead, giving him reasons why he should stay. Despite my objections he puts on his luggers and laces them up. With me close behind, he opens the door. Blanta is on the other side of it, with an old, rather doddery-looking seer, her nephew Farun, and a crowd of curious dwellers. Halfway up the north hill stand two strangers, taller than anyone in Katannya. Their skin is very pale, their eyes, shining like golden liquid, lock onto mine. Perhaps they're from another settlement.

"Seer," Blanta says, "this is the boy I told you about. He is living with the girl Arien."

"We can't have that," replies the seer. He grabs Radol's arm, hauls him out of the dwelling, and hands him over to two dwellers. The old man isn't as doddery as he appears. Radol resists, but is slim as a reed compared to the dwellers. The seer points his magic staff towards Radol then the sky, as if enlisting the help of the gods. The two men drag Radol away.

"No!" I shout, dumbfounded at what just happened.

"Don't separate us. Let me go," he yells, but they pull him through the new blades of ducan. He leaves a long smear of grass and earth as he struggles and kicks.

"I'll come back for you, Arien, never fear," he yells.

But I do fear. "We're not living together. I slept in my room, Radol in the loft," I say to the seer, trying not to sob. "We've done nothing wrong."

"It is against Katannyan guidelines for two unmarried young people to live in the same dwelling," the seer continues. "Whether they share a room or not is immaterial to —"

"A guideline is not a law," I interrupt, surprised at my own daring. One doesn't gainsay seers. This one could snap my neck with a single blow of his staff. I don't care. I'm desperate.

"It's as good as," the seer says mildly, as Radol disappears over the crest of the hill with his powerful captors. I cling grimly to the door latch in case anyone tries to take me too. I know full well it won't be to where Radol ends up. They'll keep us apart. We might never see each other again.

"You can't take Radol. You can't. He's all I have." Someone is sobbing, not me but a woman in the crowd, someone who knows my family well. She, at least, feels sympathy for me.

"There is another, more serious matter," Farun says, stepping forward. He smiles slimily at the seer as he rubs his hands together.

"What would that be?" asks the seer.

Farun nods to his aunt, who speaks out so everyone can hear. "The girl's parents were killed in an ice-turned-to-water accident. My burden beast, which I generously let them borrow, went down at the same time. The girl owes me for the loss of it. Without it I am helpless." She pauses for a second. "I claim her dwelling and lands as restitution."

I gasp. Perhaps they were planning this all along. Could it be that Farun actually pushed my parents through the ice on the lake so he and Blanta could claim my inheritance? If so, the burden beast probably never went into the water, and is hidden in Blanta's barn. She likely has the grain also. "Murderers," I want to yell. "Murderers and thieves both." But if I do, things may go even worse for me. The seer, after all, might be in Farun's pay.

"Restitution is the law — not a guideline by any means. So be it," decrees the seer, though he seems uncomfortable. Perhaps he is as guilty as they.

"How can one old burden beast be worth my family's dwelling and all our land? It's not a fair exchange. You're cheating me. Besides, if you look in her barn you'll probably find the beast."

The seer ignores me. "She may be loudmouthed and disobedient, but she has to live somewhere. Does anyone wish to adopt this girl?" He looks around. Nobody moves, which is hardly surprising, given his public assessment of me. The wind sighs through the skytrees, which are singing of longing and loss.

"We have too many children of our own," a woman calls out. "And not enough food for any of them."

"My son died during Icer," says a man, nodding in agreement. He looks skeletal, his neck thin as a flutterer's, and I wonder why his head doesn't collapse onto his shoulders.

"Perhaps the girl could replace him," the seer suggests. "Sometimes a new child eases the pain of loss."

"He died of starvation, seer. The same would likely happen to her if we took her in."

Afterwards there is only an uneasy silence.

"You, Josha? You, Donel?" the seer asks, turning to faces in the crowd he recognizes.

They shake their heads.

"What about you, Anvella? I saw you crying just now."

"Arien's mother was a good friend of mine, and I feel very sorry for the girl, but there's no way we can cope with another mouth to feed. We already have five, including the twins, and times are lean."

"My father helped you all build your dwellings and bring in your harvest-fruits. My mother helped you thatch your roofs and shared our grain with you when we had some. They were on a trekken to find food for the whole settlement when they were killed. Is there no pity in anyone?"

They look shamed, but not a sound issues from their lips. Instead they avoid my gaze, staring in an unfocused way at their toes or into the distance, to where Edge casts its ominous shadow. A man scratches his head as if trying to find a solution to the problem. I'm so angry that if I had the strength I'd shove him and everyone else across Edge into Oscura.

"She must be taken to the marketplace, then, and sold as a baseborn to whoever wants her." The seer sighs, as if the weight of his decision hangs heavy on him.

"No, for love of home and hearth, I beg you, no." I've heard stories of sold girls, forced into unspeakable acts or beaten almost to death. One baseborn was even found battered and killed in a field two cycles ago when Farlis melted the snow. The girl's owner faced no punishment. He could do what he liked with her, as she was his property. Baseborns, especially baseborn girls, aren't considered persons. They have no rights.

"Katannya is a cruel, cruel place," I cry, never before having considered what I now see to be the truth. For the most part, knowing nothing else, I've accepted the way things are. That's because the decisions of the seers seemed to have nothing to do with me. I've seen others suffer, to be sure, but remained aloof, cocooned, safe at home with my parents. But no more. I feel horribly exposed, as if I'm standing naked in the middle of Katannya's market square. "How brutish our laws are," I say bitterly. "And I don't know why I have to be called baseborn when I'm not."

"Because you are like a baseborn, orphaned, with no means to support yourself," the seer says, beginning to lose patience. "That is how we describe your plight."

"I have no means because you've stolen my inheritance," I say boldly.

"I have ruled according to our laws and traditions. You no longer have a family. You have no dwelling. You have no food. This way, at least, you may survive."

"I'm still not baseborn. I was well born to parents who loved me. The seers have too many stupid laws."

"We are the instruments of the gods. The gods decree that those abandoned must be found homes of one kind or another. It is a good law."

"I don't believe in the gods. If they really existed they wouldn't have let my parents die in such a dreadful way, leaving me alone." Though I'm past caring what he might do to me, my words surprise even me. The dwellers around me gasp.

"You are beginning to irritate me. That's enough. The gods hear everything you say. They may strike you dead when you least expect it, to punish you for your evil words."

"I am punished enough already," I say quietly, very sad, very sorry for myself.

"Silence." The seer points his staff at me, signalling an end to the dialogue.

The two tall strangers have disappeared, but the dwellers have grown more numerous, drawn by the commotion. People mill around, muttering to one another; I even hear someone laughing. How disgusting, to make merry at my expense. Nevertheless, I start to laugh too. Mirth bubbles up inside me at the ludicrousness of my situation; however, most dwellers are shocked, either by what I've said about the gods, or by my laughter. They put their hands to their foreheads or cover their ears, awaiting retribution. They peer through their fingers at the heavens, expecting me and perhaps all of them to be struck dead by a lightning bolt. I stop laughing immediately. I almost expect retribution too. When no lightning is forthcoming, however, I stand straight and kick those whose hands reach forward to disentangle my fingers from the door latch. I hurt myself more than I hurt anyone else. My feet are bare.

"I don't have my luggers on," I cry, in a final feeble protest. "Let me fetch them."

"So you can kick us harder?" retorts a scar-faced man.

"No. So my feet aren't cut on the sharp stones and lingering shards of ice scattered in the fields." If I could just slip into the dwelling, perhaps I could escape by a back window or door while they wait for me at the front. I could jump from the second floor. I've done so in the past. But no one is listening to me. No one, not even the seer, says yes or no. No one is left who cares whether I go barefoot to the market or feels sorry that my parents are dead, and Radol is taken from me. Blanta and Farun are only interested in my property, and others remain because they want to see what is to be done about me. I've become the entertainment of the moment, a buffoon for the crowd.

It begins to rain, a cold, sharp mixture of water and ice, the last dregs of Icer. Sleet attacks my skin like a thousand spikelfish needles. Dwellers start to scatter and the old seer is soaked. After wiping his face on his sleeve, he takes a thin rope from his pouch. Placing his staff under his arm he binds my hands behind my back. He explains that this is the custom in such cases. No doubt he's had enough of both the weather and me. He wants to go home. My heart beats too fast, my knees buckle, I go down.

"I have you, Arien," gloats Farun, seizing me as I fall. He slings me over his shoulder like a sack of gulrid grain. I smell his skein of rancid, oily hair, his noxious sweat, the stench of which is intensified by the wetness of his tunic..

"Take her to the market place," orders the seer.

Farun moves fast, up and over the brow of the north hill. He skids twice on the muddy ground. Each time, my face and chest bump hard against his back and I groan. Laughing at my discomfort, he carries me away from my life.

CHAPTER FIVE

I'm standing in the market for the fourth day, my bare feet tied together with leather thongs. With effort I can stay balanced, but I can't walk without falling over.

No one has shown any interest in claiming or buying me, though dwellers barter at the stalls for the few foodstuffs available. Caged flutterers and grunts are not there, all those bound for market having been eaten during Icer. Some of the sellers are gone too, having nothing left to trade. The marketplace is more than half empty. The prices of foodstuffs that remain are high, only the wealthy able to afford them. Apart from an occasional sleight-of-hand boy, who makes off with whatever he can eat, the poor nurse their hunger at home until harvest, when more may be available.

It looks as though no one can afford *me* with the price of grain what it is. Food, after all, is a necessity. I'm not, unless someone takes it into his head to eat me. That's a joke — hopefully. Perhaps I'll stay here till I rot. I imagine myself trodden underfoot, ground into dust.

Anvella has taken pity on me today. She brings water, her children trailing behind her, and places a log on the cobbles. "Thank you." I gulp the liquid before sitting, still hot and miserable, on the log. My eyes smart with exhaustion. I close them, seeing the red sun of Farlis through my eyelids. The sun is burning through my hair and the skin of my head. It is singeing my brain. Solar will come fast this cycle.

"I'll bring you more water tomorrow, and a hat," promises Anvella, as she leaves.

"May the gods bless you," I croak.

"I'll take the girl," a voice calls out behind me. "I need a baseborn for my new dwelling. She can help my aunt."

I open my eyes. It's Farun. I totter back up, furious. "It isn't enough that you turn me out. Now you think you can force me back into my own home as your slave. Perhaps I can sleep in Blanta's barn with your burden beast, you murderer. I'm sure you still have it."

Farun doesn't bother to contradict me. "How much do you want for her?" he asks Keeper, the baseborns' guard, as he jingles quoinies in his pouch. "I've had some profitable dealings recently. I can afford twenty-five quoinies."

It's a pittance. I'm apparently worth less than a measure of grain.

Well aware that he's attempting to pay for me with some of the money that should rightfully be mine — it probably came from the quick sale of a parcel of my parents' land — I point it out. "I'll die before I let you buy me," I add angrily. "I'll stuff my mouth with poisonous horn berries."

"None to be had in early Farlis." He grins. "Nor toad berries neither."

I try to clout him, would kill him if I could. But because of the shackles I trip instead, grazing my knees so my blood runs orange. Nobody takes any notice of my bleeding legs, stinging grit embedded in them, as I scramble to get up. That's because, for the most part, baseborns are invisible.

I used to pass by children or youths for sale in the marketplace without qualm or concern, even if they were only three or four cycles old. Indeed, I felt superior to them, as if it was their fault they were forced to stand at the market waiting for bidders. It shames me now to think of it. But "it is our way," as the seer who ordered me here would say, and until recently I didn't question what *our way* really means — a sticky web to capture and enslave the helpless. It never once occurred to me, shopping in the market with my mother, that I could become entangled in that web myself. After all, I was loved. I was cared for. In my thoughtless arrogance I believed I deserved a good life while those children did not. How fearful they must have felt as misfortune entrapped them, and life as they had understood it was ripped away. They had become cheap goods, tradable or disposable — as had I — through no fault of their own.

"If I were to take a guess, I'd say you have designs on her." Keeper winks as he smirks at Farun.

"Not so," replies Farun. But he is smirking too.

"She's a spirited one and no mistake."

"I'll break her, never fear."

"What's your best offer?" Keeper scratches his back and under his arms. "Remember that the money goes to the seers for the good of the settlement."

"Right, and of course you don't benefit by it," Farun says sarcastically. "Thirty quoinies is my limit." He counts the coins and holds them out.

"Not nearly enough to snag her," snarls Keeper.

"Like you've had other offers."

The two of them continue to bicker about price, their faces red as lush-fruit, their voices rising in the stifling air. I hide behind my eyes and try to imagine pleasant events, a Farlis ride along a singing river, a swim in a safe limpid pool with Radol. It doesn't work. Their voices, like the squabbled-over quoinies, rattle my brain.

"Quiet, dwellers. Stop your prattle."

Farun and Keeper don't hear the newcomer, or if they do they take no notice. They are still arguing, their faces red, their voices ever more raucous and mean. The man who has just arrived shouts out sharply, his voice drowning out their din. Powerfully built, he carries a long stave. It's made from a thick vine twined around a straight branch, with what appears to be an eye carved into the head of it. He is a seer, there can be no doubt of it, because of his ornate stave, his rich purple cassock, his commanding air. He is also clearly accustomed to being obeyed. Farun and Keeper desist.

"I am Yaddair, Chief Seer of Vor. I wish to see the girl that you have. A wayfarer at our settlement told me that she was in the marketplace of Katannya, her parents dead. There is a dearth of females for sale at present, and I need one, so I trekkened hither."

"She is right here, Chief Seer Yaddair." Keeper, who is no doubt calculating what he might get for me from the rich seer, bows low. Rising and prodding my shoulder, he forces me to totter forward, one tiny step at a time so I don't fall again.

I take a shuddering breath. My thoughts fly back and forth in knotty confusion. Yaddair is the Chief Seer of Vor, so he says, and I have no reason to doubt him. Is that good or bad for me? Vor is closer to Edge than Katannya, much closer, the closest settlement to Oscura. It is also further north, will be foggier, darker, colder in Icer than it is here. It will almost certainly travel me farther from Radol. But seers and their families live well. If Yaddair wants to buy me and he's a reasonable master, I will probably get enough to eat and a comfortable place to sleep. More than that I might want but can't hope for.

Even with the prospect of decent food, the thought of Yaddair purchasing me makes me uneasy and nauseated, but it's nowhere near as frightening as imagining Farun dragging me back to what I still consider my own dwelling. I don't like the way he stares at me or licks his fat greasy lips, touching or grabbing me whenever and wherever he can, as if he can't wait to be my owner. He said he'd break me, as if I'm a disobedient beast, and I dread the methods he might use to do so. And Blanta, if she gets half a chance, will surely work me to death.

Yaddair turns away from the two men, but the eye at the top of his stave glares at them. They look discomfited. It blinks twice and they don't move so much as a finger from then on, or at least, not unless told to.

"I am interested in this baseborn," Yaddair says, turning back. "I have, after all, come a long way to see her. I hope she's worth the journey. Open your mouth, girl, so I can examine your teeth."

I feel like a milk beast but do as he bids me.

"Hm. Now show me your hands."

"Yes, Seer Yaddair." I'd furled them into fists at the men's bickering. I open them tentatively and hold them out, still chilblained from Icer. He turns them over so he can see my reddened palms, which I've tried to hide from him.

"You seem like a good strong girl with your wits about you. Although your hands are delicate, the line across your palms together with the patches of rough skin indicate a hard worker. The lines that descend to your wrists and wrap around them tell me you will have a long life."

"Thank you, Seer Yaddair." I'm relieved to hear that I can expect to live long. If the seer is right, I won't starve, or get beaten to death like that poor girl in the snow-swept field. And I might be able to work my way out of the situation I now find myself in.

"How old are you?"

"Fifteen cycles, Seer Yaddair. Almost."

"I would have put you younger. You're a tiny little crea-ture, to be sure. But I get the feeling you're stronger than you look. We could use your help with the children, and with the gathering of grain at harvestime. First Wife has been very tired recently: too many hard Icers with not enough respite."

I nod to show I understand, but in fact I don't. First Wife? How many wives does he have? Will I be expected to work for all of them? I'm worried, but there's no disobeying him. He won't be mild with me if I do. I see it in his eyes, in the creases of his forehead, and in his long, thin nose, which looks capable of smelling out any wrongdoing. I see it in the way he deals with Farun and Keeper. Most important of all, I see it in his stave, which appears to be alive, its one eye glaring fiercely.

Like all of the more impressive seers, Yaddair moves with a sense of his own importance that is no doubt shored up by his people. They must believe — as our dwellers do of our seers — that he communes with the gods. Only he knows for sure whether that's true. But he isn't like that foolish old man, the Katannyan seer fit for retirement, who even though he had the last word, was content to let me argue with him. Yaddair appears all-powerful, and I can see he's accustomed to absolute obedience, to getting what he wants without argument. What he wants at the moment is me. I can only hope that if he gets me he will treat me reasonably.

"Do you wish to come with me, girl?"

This is a surprise. I didn't expect to be asked for my opinion, to have the freedom to decide for myself what I want, as if I'm still a real person. I weigh Yaddair against Farun, as if they're on opposing sides of a gulrid-grain balance. Although I barely know the seer, I'm sure I was right in thinking he was a better choice than Farun. And now he's actually consulted me, so he must care what I think and want. "Yes, Seer Yaddair," I reply. "I wish to come with you."

"Good. I should hate to be disappointed after such a long trekken." As Yaddair turns to bargain with Keeper, Farun spits on me. Sickened, I wipe his saliva off my face.

"I will pay you two quoinies," Yaddair tells Keeper, as he produces them. They're worth almost nothing.

Keeper hesitates. "Excuse me Chief Seer Yaddair," he says, "but the other man was willing to … uh … give me thirty …"

"So you prefer to give her to him?"

"No, Chief Seer. I was just wondering if …" His voice sputters and dies. He doesn't bite the quoinies either, as he would with anybody else, to test whether they're real. He just jiggles the two coins in his hand until they catch the light, before nodding his acceptance.

"And for your trouble," says the seer, "I promise Katannya a good harvest."

"Thank you, Seer Yaddair," says Keeper, lifting his palms to his forehead and bowing again, despite the fact he's just lost twenty-eight of the thirty quoinies he'd have got from Farun if the seer hadn't shown up. "I am honoured to do business with you."

"Get this girl a decent pair of luggers and cut the thongs that bind her. We have two days' travel ahead of us."

Keeper bows again, cuts me loose, measures my feet against his hand, and hurries off to find luggers, muttering as he goes. They will cost him all of the two quoinies he received from Yaddair. Farun, looking furious in defeat, vanishes over the hill towards home. *My* home.

CHAPTER SIX

"We are close to my home at last," Yaddair tells me one evening.

I'm hot and dirty after days of travel. I've tried to memorize our way to Vor, so that if I can ever escape I can find my way back. Though it occurs to me that there's nothing left to go back *for*, I still note interesting features as we walk: past a huge flutterer nest, through a valley between high hills, over an outcropping that we sleep on, a forest of tall green and red skytrees that offer us their unfamiliar fruit. We also spend days walking through fields and pasture land, passing two small settlements on our way, Ashor and Loden. The dwellings are all shut up. No one greets us. A long vermilion snake emerges from the forest and hisses at us, wrapping itself tightly around my ankle. Its head rears up. Seer Yaddair knocks it off me with his stave, slicing it in half with a sharp knife he carries in his belt. The front half slithers away. "Very poisonous!" he remarks. "Very hard to destroy." I don't doubt it, but am too stunned to cry. For the most part the animals and plants leave us alone afterwards. It occurs to me that they fear for their lives when they see him.

The weather has grown ever more cold and foggy as we've trekkened. The sky is muddy green, very different from the brilliant skies of Katannya. It doesn't change colour as we reach Vor. My feet are so swollen I can barely fasten my new luggers; my hips ache so badly I wonder if my legs will break. I slide down into a sitting position, my back against a zigzag tree. It is as sharp-angled as a starving drog and it neither waves its branches nor sings. It just creaks as if annoyed, suggesting impolitely that I should move.

"Stand back up," Yaddair says, "and look beyond those zigzags. The main settlement is out of sight, but my home isn't." He sighs. I'm not sure whether this means he's glad to be back or not. The tree pokes me hard with a crooked finger. I can hear it thinking, *I'll kill her, see if I don't, when he's not around.* I jump up in alarm. But Yaddair has heard nothing.

"This is Seersland, girl," he says, "the part of Vor that belongs to me as Chief Seer." He points towards a series of dismal-looking buildings sprawled over veiled, misty fields.

"I have never seen its like. There is no dwelling half as big in Katannya."

"We call it the castrel. It is by far the biggest dwelling in Vor, perhaps the biggest on Lightside."

He's proud of it, I can tell. How important Yaddair must be to live in the castrel, as he calls it. He must be important for another reason too: He has more than one wife. Men in Katannya never have two. The seer has spoken on our trek-ken of First Wife, Neretta — of how clever and resourceful she is when her bones aren't aching and her mouth is closed.

He adds that he can't tell her anything important, as she can no more keep silent about it than stop eating. I'm surprised he speaks so freely about her to me, especially as he doesn't mention Second or any other wife he might have. Then I realize: Baseborns are expected to be silent as the dead about those they labour for. Speaking to a baseborn should be like speaking to oneself. Any word heard by her is to be disregarded, or at least never passed on to others for fear of severe reprisal. Or death.

Yaddair is on the move again, striding towards the castrel. The fields, or wolds as he calls them, though hazy, appear to stretch all the way to Edge, where they're swallowed up in a forbidding, ash-coloured fog. Just before we arrive I catch sight of something that must be a smokie, like those of Ongis. Then another. Plumes of steam rising from them melt into the fog. There's no bright fire drifting from their craters. We're so close to Oscura that I imagine all the dark corners that must exist both in the castrel and the rest of Vor, places where the dusty sun can hide. I turn away from Edge and move fast because it frightens me to be anywhere near it. Yaddair has entered the castrel and I move even faster, despite my blistered feet, following him into a huge steamy cookroom.

"Another young girl? Will you take this one to your bed too?"

This must be Neretta, the wife who can't keep her mouth shut. I gasp, both at her hostile tone and her insinuations.

"What kind of greeting is this? I bring you a servant, to help you in your daily chores, and this is how you treat me? Quiet, old woman."

"May the gods forgive you, old man."

I'm standing between them, the apparent cause of their enmity. I wish to be anywhere on Kondar except here. I want to hide. Yaddair's eyes burn like fire. He puts his arm around me, but I recoil, terrified of his touch after what's been said. I am for Radol, and Radol is for me, no matter how long we have to wait.

"Come, Arien. You have no reason to fear. Two wives are quite enough for me. More than enough, most days." It's the first time he's called me by name. His use of it isn't calming. It pricks like the poisonous thorns of a horn-berry bush. "I saved you from the market," he continues. "I've not been anything but kind to you, isn't that right? I would never hurt you. *In any way.*"

"I know, Seer Yaddair." But my fears are not diminished. His kindness no longer comforts me because I see the possible scheming that feeds it.

"You can sleep in the barn out yonder, baseborn," Neretta informs me, a sour look on her face. She appears to want me as far from her — and perhaps from *him* — as possible.

"Nonsense!" Yaddair throws his stave down in the corner. Its eye blinks then shuts. "She can't sleep on dried ducan with the milk-beasts and drogs. The girl sleeps in the castrel with pillow and quilt like everyone else."

"To my mind she should be locked out of here at night. On your head be it if she steals from us — or worse — when we're asleep." Grumbling about her painful knees, Neretta, lips set in a thin line of disgust, takes me to find somewhere that will meet with her husband's approval. The castrel, though unappealing on the outside, is magnificent within. It possesses room after room, all of which lead off one another through winding hallways and up to different floors. It's like a fur-beast warren. At least twenty or more dwellers could fit into it comfortably. Mother would say it's a waste of space. But she would be envious, all the same.

We take two stairways, one that goes up and one down again after a long stretch of corridor and several twisty turns. We stop halfway down the second set of stairs, on a landing. Neretta takes a key from her belt and opens the door to a small room containing a bed, a window, but not much else. Second Wife, I'm told, sleeps next door with her child. I'm not on any account to disturb them.

"Go to sleep," Neretta says nastily, without offering me any food. She looks me up and down before snorting with contempt. After she leaves I push my bed against the door for safety, just in case Yaddair should take it into his head to visit me. I lie down, too anxious to close my eyes. Much later I hear a baby's sharp wail. It slices through the silence of the night. A woman whom I assume to be Second Wife starts to cry too. I hear her through the wall. "Shut up!" she yells at the baby. Then "What have I done?" she sobs. "Why am I here?" Nobody answers. I feel a momentary kinship with Second Wife.

CHAPTER SEVEN

Her name is Gilan. She looks to be around my age and is strikingly beautiful, with thick, flowing hair that reaches past her waist and gleams silver. Despite her appearance, I have no idea why Yaddair took it into his mind to marry her. She can't or won't sew or cook, and — this is what I find most astonishing — she won't take care of her own baby; she hardly ever picks him up, and seems helpless around him. Neretta constantly shouts at her, but it makes no difference. She doesn't appear to know or want to know one end of him from the other, and simply sits and stares into the distance then weeps when he soils himself, needs feeding, or when Neretta chastises her. "I have tried every remedy I've ever mixed on you," First Wife says. "Nothing seems to work."

"That's because I spit it out."

"I have a mind to poison your food with toad berries," Neretta snarls.

"That *will* please Yaddair," Gilan says sarcastically, before yawning in Neretta's face.

"The old man's fancy will ruin us all," Neretta complains when her husband is absent. As well as being riled by Gilan's behaviour, she is likely jealous. I'd like to feel triumphant, but though I thoroughly dislike her, despise her at times, I can't help but feel sorry for her. What can be worse than to have one's place in the family usurped by someone younger and prettier? "And you," she goes on. "Has he visited your room yet, in the middle of the night?"

"No, nor could he. I set my bed against the door to keep everyone out while I sleep. But from what I've learnt about him, I can't believe he'd do any such thing. He is kind and fatherly towards me, nothing more. And he doesn't go into Gilan's room either. I'm sure I'd hear him if he did."

"Hmph. Then why would he wed such a useless, wicked lump of lard and bring her here? Was he out of his mind? I should beat some sense into her." The next day, she gossips with dweller wives about the problem and asks their advice as we all sit quilting.

"Harshness," says one. "Harshness is the answer. Make her understand once and for all who's in charge."

"I agree," says another. "A taste of the whip soon chastens a willful beast."

Neretta has apparently taken the women's words to heart. After they've gone, she hits Gilan hard across the face when the girl refuses to feed her baby. The punishment doesn't work. Gilan fights back, biting Neretta on the ear and yanking her hair until she screams. I grab the baby from the bed and crouch behind a table trying to shield him. My action is not entirely unselfish. I don't want to be pitched into the fray myself.

Neretta shrieks again, yanks Gilan's hair several times, scratches her face, and kicks her in the belly, but there's no question that because she's older and weaker she gets the worst of the exchange. After the battle, bunches of silver and brown hair lie on the floor. Most of it is brown, coiled like a slither of snakes.

"Clean the mess up immediately," Neretta says to me, seething with rage, "before Yaddair gets home." When she turns away I notice a bare patch on the back of her head, which she luckily doesn't know about. Busy with the baby, I forget to clean up the hair. I'm punished for it later, obliged to go to bed with no supper.

"I have two children of my own, as you well know, and have looked after them myself with no help from anyone," Neretta tells Gilan next day. "In fact, when I birthed my girls, there *was* no one to help." Gilan ignores her. She is drawing intricate patterns on her arms with green dye.

Neretta is so incensed that she turns puce and a small vessel bursts in her cheek. Blood trickles down her face. Feeling something amiss she puts her hand to the spot then examines her fingertips. Her blood is the same colour as Gilan's green dye. While Gilan's own blood is a kind of spangly white, the colour of bitter-fruit — I saw it when cleaning up the rags from her periodic bleed — Neretta's shows that her female ancestors belonged to a royal house long since vanished. This doesn't mean that Gilan respects her any more for it. "Now we match," she crows victoriously, as her rival rushes out of the room, alarmed, to patch up her face. "Your blood with my dye." I leave in Neretta's wake, cradling the baby to my chest to keep him safe.

Yaddair knows, I'm sure, that the two wives hate each other intensely, but as Chief Seer, it appears he has more important matters to attend to, though as to what they might be, I have no inkling. Women, although they may be carriers of important bloodlines, seemingly have little else to recommend them, so are never informed of what transpires in Council or anywhere else. The thoughts of the seers are obviously considered too lofty for female minds to grasp.

Without being told, however, I feel in my bones that something is badly amiss. Yaddair's frown lines grow deeper as the days pass. He cannot settle when he's at home, and I know he can't sleep, as I hear him pacing in the middle of the night, the floorboards in his backroom downstairs creaking. The sound carries to my room, which is directly above his. I have no idea why he's so restless, but it's not my place to ask. His problems, though, intersect with my own, because I rely on his good offices to keep me alive.

He almost always leaves his twisted stick behind when he goes away. Perhaps he needs it to watch over his wives to ensure murder isn't committed while he's gone, though much of the fighting goes on upstairs. Gilan rarely ventures down. In any case, he's careful with the stave and places it upright in the cookroom corner before slipping through the door. The eye shuts while he's out, opens when he returns. It stares left and right, or up at the ceiling and down at the floor. When the eye moves, I hear a peculiar scratching sound, a ghostly echo that frightens me until I realize what's causing it.

A few days after my arrival, Miko the baby becomes almost entirely my charge. Gilan has retired to a couch studded with rainbow gems in her room. The walls are hung with colourful tapestries. The room is the only brightly decorated spot in the castrel, likely in the whole of Vor. She idles the days away as she spreads perfumed oils on her face and hands and braids her hair after combing grunt butter through it. She wears soft, narrow slippers. I can't imagine her ever wearing luggers. Even though I'm small and thin, I feel clumsy as a milk beast next to her. I have to admit it: I don't have grace. But at least my life is far more useful than hers, and that gives me a perverse sense of satisfaction.

Each feeding time, I remove the baby from his make-shift sling across my shoulder and give him to Gilan. I put him to her breast to feed, but she doesn't put her arms around him. She shies away as if he's deformed, so I must continue to hold him as he sucks. Afterwards I take him with me as I go about my chores. He's quite a weight to haul around, but as I sweep or scrub, I'm glad of his company. He's someone to talk to even if, except for his babbling, he isn't yet up to answering.

At first I'm hopeful I might make a friend of Gilan, as the girl is even more unhappy than I am and we're so close in age, but she resists all attempts at conversation, remaining silent as she examines her fingernails for dirt or slides her comb through her hair. She ignores my presence unless she wants something, while continuing to weep almost every day and most nights. Her weeping alters the fabric of my dreams.

"Come now, stop," I say one morning after her staring into space is replaced by a new storm of tears. "You have a lovely place to live, good food to eat, and a baby who loves you. If you're lonely and sad, honoured mistress, we could be friends."

"Friends with a baseborn?" she sneers, the sole words she has ever addressed to me.

"I was born into a good house with noble blood and parents who loved me, as I'm sure you were. Because you keep crying, your swollen eyes are marring your beauty," I say in a feeble attempt to stop her. Gilan growls, stops sobbing, and flings her comb at me. Although badly wanting to, I resist flinging it back. She lies on her side and greases her hair.

Days are so taken up by hard work there's little opportunity for thinking. As soon as Neretta sees I can cope with the chores she's given me, she piles on more. According to her, she had to do it all before I came, so she's not asking me to do anything she hasn't done herself. I'm obliged to climb a nearby hill every day, carrying a heavy pot to fetch water from the nearby stream. Every other day I wash the family's clothes at the dead pool where all the laundry is done. The other women there must know I'm baseborn. Though they're on friendly terms with one another, they either ignore me, or lapse into silence and stare at me as I work. I labour until my arms and legs ache so badly I can barely drag myself back to the castrel.

As if that's not enough, Neretta complains about how fast the harvestime grain is disappearing, accusing me of stealing it. But she can have no evidence because there isn't any. I've never touched so much as a mouthful of it and am quick to tell her so.

I long desperately for night so I can rest my bones. Nights, though, in their way, are worse. Alone in my room, I picture my parents constantly before I drift off to sleep. I remember Father taking me down to Icer Lake to look at the small lives that dwelt under a rock by the shore. How could we know then that death awaited him there? I shake my brain clear of tragedy to think of happier times; I recall my mother teaching me how to make tiny cakes from gulrid grain and hushberries for Gloonisdeg, the new-cycle celebration of the return of Farlis.

I've also begun to make friends with Neretta's twin daughters, playing with them whenever I have a free moment. I love it when we play catch-as-catch-can. The girls run away, flapping their arms like demented flutterers. It's not hard to find them: they squeal and squabble. When I've caught them, I swing them around and tickle them till they scream with laughter.

They ease my loneliness. But all too soon my thoughts become melancholy again: I think of Radol every evening, wondering where the dwellers took him and whether, unlike me, he's free. We used to play catch-as-catch-can as well as hide-and-find when we were children too, but I doubt we'll ever meet again.

Sometimes I wake with a start and stare out of my window, shocked that I'm in Vor, that I've lost the one person remaining who is dear to me. Even my friendship with the little girls cannot make up for my loss. One evening I prick the outline of Radol's name onto my forearm with a sharp needle. I steal a little of Gilan's dye and rub it across his name so it will stay, so I will always have something to remember him by. The dye mixes with the droplets of blood freed by the piercing. It burns brown and I stuff my hand into my mouth. But unlike Gilan's noisy crying or the twins' squealing, my tears are silent, almost non-existent. As I used to say when I was a small child, "I'm crying in my mind."

Often fog mars the settlement, the gardens and high wolds a dirty grey instead of the violet skies, red-green sky-trees, and brilliant flowers that are familiar to me. I'm even nostalgic for the white, white snow of Katannya now I'm far from it. The snow that covers Seersland is the same grimy colour as everything else. "What am I doing in this cold place?" I ask myself when I catch sight of the dreariness outside. I want to go backward in time so I'm sitting by the fire in Katannya with Mother and Father. I want to travel far, far back to the time before they died, so I can warn them before they go through the ice. I tell the girls and even the baby stories about my life. Beklee and Yanna listen attentively. The baby chuckles when he's not sucking his fingers.

Of course life can't go into reverse, however much I want it to. Sometimes I feel Edge closing in on me. Even my dreams have become more poisonous than they ever were before. I have a slightly different recurring nightmare in Vor than in Katannya, of jagged leaden clouds with slimy ice-rain pelting down from them. Loathsome shadowy creatures in black rags thrash around on the sodden ground, moaning horribly. Sometimes I become one of the creatures, fearful, sick, dying. That's when I wake up. Once as I awoke I was screaming.

"Stop your baseborn screeching!" Gilan yelled through the wall. Now she's spoken to me twice.

CHAPTER EIGHT

Miko the baby is soon weaned. I named him Miko because it suited his round, milky face. Besides, no one else had bothered to think up anything to call him. Everyone refers to him as Miko now, except for Gilan, who doesn't refer to him at all. He has a throaty chortle that I love. I make silly faces so he chortles more.

The first Solar I'm in Vor he begins to crawl and then almost immediately to run — he has missed out walking altogether — and I have to chase him all over Seersland. He constantly falls, grazing knees and elbows and leaking yellow blood. I clean it up before Neretta sees it, as his wounds would just be something else to chastise me for. The other children have also become more and more my responsibility. At harvestime, they rush away in different directions to hide from me. They're constantly disappearing behind trees or into fields of tall grain. They're used to playing with me and expect me to chase them all the time. "I'm too busy," I say. "I have to help your father's workers with the gathering and threshing of the grain."

"What grain?" asks Yanna, disappointed.

"The grain from the wold. Gulrid grain. It's right there in front of you."

I'm new to threshing but am instructed by a man named Milar, who is kind and patient, never shouting at me or ridiculing my ignorance. It's a relief to have someone pleasant to speak to. Others start to talk to me too, taking their cue from Milar.

Icer arrives far too fast. It's my job to dig the castrel out when the snow falls so deep that the family can't get through the door. Not that anyone would want to for more than five minutes, with the exception of Yaddair, who still goes down to the Council House, and the twins, who love Icer so much they'd freeze to death if I didn't keep my eyes on them constantly. I let Miko crawl around and eat snow for a few minutes before returning him to the castrel so I can finish my work.

I'm exhausted from the constant shovelling, but dare not cross Neretta; it's too dangerous: She, like Gilan, has a temper. So I say nothing, though most days my fingers are stiff with cold and my nose stuffed with ice. Yaddair, returning from a meeting one particularly cold and snowy day, takes pity on me.

"Come into the house and warm yourself by the fire." He tucks my arm in his and leads me inside. I have long since learned not to be suspicious of him, and welcome the warmth of his arm in its fur sleeve. My fingers and toes are so frozen I can hardly feel them. "Look at you," he goes on. "Your cheeks are caked with hail. Soon, if you're not careful, you'll freeze into a statue." He turns to Neretta angrily.

"It is your job to look after the castrel and treat everyone here in a fair and humane way. You are not supposed to work Arien to death. She is to be treated as a member of the household."

"Member of the household indeed!" Neretta laughs. "Orphans are expendable when they're not profitable. But if you hadn't brought that other girl, Gilan the do-nothing bride, into the house, I wouldn't have to work the baseborn so hard … or are you still planning to take this one into your bed too?"

"Shut your mouth, old woman. I have no time for your stupid, uncalled-for jealousies. There is a crisis in the Council that I've been addressing, or I would have noticed your harsh treatment of the girl much earlier. Just do what you're told and look after her as if she's your own. Give some of the heavier work to my men to do. That way, you won't come to harm." He picks up his stave from the cook-room corner, bangs it twice on the floor, and vanishes into the small room at the back of the house. His pacing room, as I call it. As he goes, the eye snaps open and fixes Neretta with an evil glare.

"A crisis?" cries Neretta, wringing her hands. "There's a crisis? What can the old man possibly mean? And why am I never told what's happening?"

"Because you can't keep your mouth shut," I whisper to myself, remembering Yaddair's earlier words about her.

But it isn't long before she finds out. No more than a handful of moments later the drogs in the barn begin to snarl and yawp. At the same time there is a loud rapping, so loud, in fact, that it shakes the spoons on the table. As I open the door, snow blows in, the gale all but extinguishing our fire. A seer, wearing the purple robes and full regalia of office, stands outside. I scarcely have time to step aside before he sweeps into the cookroom.

"Where is Yaddair, Seer of Vor?" He speaks stridently, brushing ice off his robes and stamping his feet to remove the snow from his luggers, leaving the meltings on the floor. He must have followed Yaddair from the Council House. There can be no other explanation for his appearing at the castrel so soon after Yaddair's arrival. Miko, woken abruptly from his milky dreams, starts to cry. He toddles to me and grabs hold of the fringe of my tunic. "No like it, Arin," he complains. His first sentence!

"Yaddair, *Chief* Seer of Vor, if you don't mind, Seer Morlova." Neretta draws herself up to her full height and sucks in her belly, which is no mean feat. It has never been the same since she birthed her two girls, she always tells me, her stomach jiggling like milk-beast jelly. She blames Yaddair for her extra weight.

"Chief Seer? Huh! Not for much longer," Morlova retorts. "He took the girl Gilan to wife when she was only fourteen cycles, which is against the law. Her parents recently came forward to complain after they found out she had borne a child. They say it had been agreed that the seer wouldn't touch her before she was sixteen."

"And why he should want to, I have no idea," Neretta complains.

I feel an old familiar faintness, grip the back of a chair so I don't fall. Miko sinks to the floor and rolls over. He's done with crying and chuckles as he flexes his toes.

"Nevertheless …" says the seer. He is interrupted again by Neretta.

"Old men and their stupid fancies! I told him not to bring that do-nothing into the house. Now look where it's got us." She covers her face with her hands and rocks back and forth as if mourning the death of an old friend. Gilan floats in to see what's happening. She frowns. It's the first time I've seen her out of her room in ages, but she doesn't stay, although implored by Seer Morlova to do so.

"It stinks in here," she complains. "Like rancid burden meat and old tate peelings." The long translucent train of her dress drifts along the floor behind her like the tail of a serpent.

The seer watches her train slide back out of the room as he speaks. "The Council will discuss this very serious problem and vote as soon as practical. I come here to demand that Yaddair's magic stave — his Vor badge of office — be turned over to the Council until the vote is concluded."

Neretta takes her hands from her face. "I suppose you've put your own name forward as his replacement."

"As a matter of fact, Neretta, First Wife of Yaddair, that's exactly what I've done. I am the better choice, the gods know. I don't steal babies from their mothers and put them with child."

Yaddair bangs the door of his backroom open and strides into the cookroom, twisted staff in hand. "I've been listening to your drivel, Morlova. You're not getting my stave. And you're not getting my position. Get out of my castrel. Or I'll make you. And never discuss my affairs with the women of my household again. Or with anyone else, if you know what's good for you."

"Don't you dare threaten me, Yaddair. The stave does not belong to you. Nor does the castrel. They are the property of the Chief Seer of Vor. It remains to be seen who that is," says Seer Morlova.

"Get out, I said." Yaddair jumps towards him, stave raised, but Morlova is quicker than he is. The younger seer has opened the door and ducked back into the storm. The blizzard shrieks across the cookroom and into the hall. We shiver at what's to come.

CHAPTER NINE

Apart from Miko's baby laughter and the occasional outburst from Gilan, it is all but silent in the castrel. Even Neretta's girls are subdued. Yaddair enters and leaves quietly, speaking to nobody. He puts his stave in the corner as usual, but I now realize it's not to spy on his wives, it's so that no one in the Council can appropriate it. With the stave goes the power.

Before Morlova paid us a visit, Yaddair was beginning to teach his daughters how to read and write runes. One day he caught me listening at the door. To my delight he invited me in to participate. "Girls need an education too," he said. His runes are very unlike Father's, much more elaborate. He gave me a stylus and told me that in future I was to do my best to copy what he wrote. I watched him carefully as he demonstrated each rune, trying to duplicate the complicated squiggles on the thin sheets of papertree leaves that he provided me with. "You're doing very well," he would often say. But since Morlova came calling, he's stopped teaching us. When I have a free moment, I try to teach the girls myself to keep things as normal as possible. I have them read to me. I don't teach them writing though; Yaddair's runes are too difficult.

"How long does it take the sun to revolve around Kondar?" I ask one day in what I consider to be a leaderly voice.

"Twenty-five days," Yanna says with great assurance.

"Thirty-two," replies her sister.

"You're both wrong. It takes approximately four hundred days. And it was a trick question. Kondar revolves around the sun, not the other way around. Or so the seers say. When does the New Cycle begin?" I ask.

"What's a New Cycle?" queries Beklee. "And what do the gods do with the old one?"

"Don't be silly, Becklee," says Yanna. "The gods throw the old cycle in the rubbish and take the new one out of a copburde at the beginning of Icer."

"Farlis," I correct her. "That's when we celebrate Gloonisdeg. It's not a fixed date. It varies, depending on when the snow begins to melt. How many hours in a day?"

"Ten," Yanna replies confidently.

"Fifteen," responds Beklee, scratching her nose.

"No, I'm sure it's ten."

"It's actually twenty," I tell them. "But good try."

"Impossible," contradicts Yanna. "How could we fill all those hours? We'd get bored."

Beklee nods her head in agreement.

"You're sleeping through half of them," I say, "so that you don't get bored the other half."

"In that case they can't be counted as part of the day. The answer is ten, as I already said." Yanna grins at me in catlike triumph.

I give up. They're unteachable, at least by me. I'm obviously not destined to become a leader.

Every day I clear the snow away from the front door and cut and stack mutetree wood for the fire. It's a job I enjoy doing. I've taught myself how to split wood in stages from the trunk of each tree so as not to kill it, even though the tree would be too dumb to make a fuss if I tried to. I make a horizontal opening in the trunk with my axe and begin to separate a plank from it, by making a vertical cut on either side and fixing the loosened wood open with a dead branch. As the days go by I separate the plank a little at a time with a saw until I have a long slice of wood hanging from the tree. I then remove it. Mother would say approvingly that all the sawing, separating, and stacking is toughening me up. Neretta looks after Miko while I work, although sometimes, when the weather isn't too cold or the snow too deep, I take him outside and make sure he's well clear of the axe while I chop wood. Like his older sisters, he loves snow, which is just as well, because there's plenty of it.

Sometimes Neretta actually thanks me in whispers: We've all begun to whisper to one another lately, except for the children. It's as if someone's watching us. Neretta has fashioned me a pair of hand warmers and a hood out of fur-beast skin after we ate the small creatures that first wore it. Miko also gets a pair of hand warmers, made from the beast's long ears. He tries the warmers on and claps his hands in glee. Sometimes I find him stroking the fur and babbling to it in his singsong baby talk, as if its previous owner is still alive.

Neretta's beginning, I believe, to see me as an ally rather than an enemy. She has come to realize that our lives depend on Yaddair. We both champion him even if we have reservations about what he did, so we are united against Seer Morlova, or, as Neretta has taken to calling him, *Smear All Over*. She runs the words together quickly, so that if one doesn't listen too carefully, it might sound as though she's saying his real name. The girls laugh uproariously when they hear his nickname. It lessens the tension. But still, an air of disquiet hangs around the castrel, as though something momentous is about to happen. For a time nothing does.

We have more snow than I've ever seen before in Katannya or even Vor. Icer changes late and slow into Farlis; the sun struggles its dim way out of a grey prison of fog, so that the new shoots of herbs, vegetables, and ducan can spike up through the meltings.

We have almost forgotten Seer Morlova as we go on with our daily tasks, have even begun to smile again. But he hasn't forgotten us. He returns in mid-Farlis, bringing with him an untidy gaggle of dwellers who are doing their best to appear soldierly. He bangs into the cookroom, and they shuffle in behind him.

"You are to come with me," he instructs Neretta. "And you." He waves his hand in my direction. "You are needed as witnesses in the case against Yaddair, Seer of Vor. Fetch the baby."

"He's too young to give evidence," Neretta replies with a mocking laugh.

"Watch your mouth, First Wife. Where is the victim of the crime?"

"There *is* no victim because there *was* no crime." Neretta takes Miko from the far side of the cookroom though he pushes at her arms to get free. She hands him to me before continuing. "If Yaddair were here, he would turn you out. He would set the drogs on you. He would smash you."

Morlova doesn't seem perturbed. "Yaddair is in Council to answer the charges. Where is the girl Gilan?"

Neretta and I glance at each other, then away, resolved not to answer. "Mum mum mum," gurgles Miko. It's the first time he's used the word. He points towards the ceiling, the young villain.

"Search her out," cries Morlova. "Deliver her to me." Three of the dwellers straggle up the stairs to find her. "Move," he shouts. "We don't have all day. We are about to strip Yaddair of his title, punish him once and for all for his dastardly and despicable deeds." He retrieves the stave from its corner, bellowing like a burden beast in unseersman-like triumph.

We stand in the chamber in the centre of the Council House: Neretta, Gilan, Miko, and myself. There is no ceiling to the chamber, apparently so that the spirits of the gods may enter. It also means, unfortunately, that it is open to the elements. A fine snow is falling, as if Farlis has changed its mind and gone back to bed. I can hear the roar of Edge. The building is far too close to it. Yaddair once told me that Edge was encroaching, getting closer each cycle. If we live long enough, we will be swallowed up in its fog.

I hold Miko tightly, though he squirms in my arms, as usual. He wants to be down on the ground, free to explore. Neretta told her two girls to stay home and lock the doors. Though they whimpered, she insisted that they were in no circumstances to leave the castrel until we returned. It could be dangerous. I heard them drop the latch and bolt the door behind us.

Twenty-five seers are ranged around us in the Council Chamber. I know because I counted them. Twice, needing something to occupy my mind. The dwellers who brought us in have been dismissed. Gilan has dropped to the floor and is sobbing, quietly for once. Yaddair's stave is lying in the centre of the chamber where Morlova left it. "Bring in Seer Yaddair," he barks out, a blood channel visibly swollen and ticking in his neck.

"I don't need to be brought in," says Yaddair. "I am quite capable of bringing myself in." Although we can hear his voice, we can't yet see him. I crane my neck. He enters from the back with hands folded and bows to the other seers, obliging them to bow back. In contrast to Morlova, he looks serene, comfortable, even confident, which surprises me. When he reaches the middle of the chamber, he picks up his staff and twirls it, the twists on its surface appearing to coil around the length of it like a serpent. He twirls it the other way, and the serpent uncoils and re-coils. The eye blinks. The seers draw back in fear.

"Seer Yaddair, put that stave down," commands Morlova.

"This serpentine stick belongs to the Chief Seer of Vor, and I am he."

"And as my husband says, he's *Chief* Seer Yaddair," interrupts Neretta, who knows well that her welfare and importance depend on Yaddair's position; but she speaks a little hesitantly, unlike at the castrel. She is in the Council, after all. The Council is a dangerous place. Morlova ignores her.

"Smearallover," she mutters, her lip curled.

"What was that?"

"Nothing, Seer Morlova." She fans herself with her hand. Despite the cold and snow, runnels of sweat drip down her face. There are wet patches under her arms.

"As I said, the stave belongs to me, Morlova," says Yaddair, "unless you can prove that it doesn't." He stops twirling. The eye blinks again and stares.

"I can." Morlova turns to the seers. "Seer Yaddair took a girl of fourteen cycles to wife, which is against our law. He put her with child. She lies there, prostrate with grief, while her tiny son, struggling to reach his mother, remains in the arms of the baseborn."

"Shame," cry some of the seers. "Shame, shame."

Morlova turns back to Yaddair. "You are unfit to be the Chief Seer, or for that matter, any member of the Council."

A sigh from the seers, like the soughing of the wind in the trees, is heard, followed by a deadly silence. Even Yaddair says nothing. He looks straight ahead.

"I call Gilan, Second Wife of Yaddair, to witness," Morlova commands. She stops crying but remains on the floor. Tiny grains of snow are beginning to settle on her.

"She is not fit, sir," I say, trembling at my own audacity.

"Not fit how?"

"Not fit in the way of listening or answering. She has been in despair these many seasons."

"Which proves my point. You speak for her, baseborn. Does the girl live at the castrel?"

I nod, my eyes downcast.

"Is she married to Seer Yaddair?"

"As far as I know, Seer Morlova, she is. I came when she was already living with the family."

"Is the child hers?"

I nod again, frightened though I am. Since baseborns have no standing, one wrong answer in Council could cost me my life.

"Thank you. I call Neretta, First Wife of Yaddair, to witness."

"I won't say anything in front of all these *Council* men. You'll be wasting your time," cries Neretta, clutching her throat. He questions her anyway. She doesn't respond. At last, frustrated to the point of fury, he shrieks at her to answer, for the love of the gods. She shrieks back: "Isn't this what all you men want? Silent women?"

"Obedience is what we want. Women who are gentle and timid as flutterers, women who speak when spoken to but not otherwise."

Neretta's fierce laughter echoes around the hall. "I will never grovel to you or anyone else. I will never submit to you. I will never cower before you. Never. I am First Wife to the Chief Seer of Vor. My bloodlines are pure. I am descended from the Royal women of antiquity. I say what I want when I want to. And don't you dare forget it."

"Aren't you going to question *me*?" Yaddair asks mildly.

"The case is already answered," says Morlova, red with fury.

"I think not. I am entitled to respond to the charges. Is that not so, fellow seers?"

There are a few nods. Most of the seers sit as still and silent as stones.

"Here is my testimony." Yaddair pulls a small knife from his robes. Morlova leaps forward, but before he can reach him, Yaddair slices into his own finger. Pale blue blood spurts from his wound, showing that he is descended from the ancient warriors of Kondar. "You all know how the blood-lines work. A boy's blood is the same colour as his father's."

"As girls' blood is determined by the mother's," Neretta adds.

"Exactly, First Wife. Our forebears are gone, but their blood lives on in us. Our daughters' blood is the same colour as your own. If you prick the boy's finger, you will find that his blood is *not* the same colour as mine."

"This is true. I'm the member of the household who's treated Miko's grazes often enough, and I know his blood to be yellow, not blue," I say so timidly that I'm not sure that anyone hears me.

Yaddair pauses for a moment before continuing. "His blood is not the same colour as mine because Miko *is not* my son. I'm surprised that Morlova didn't think to check this before." As he stands there, totally at ease, there is consternation in the Council Chamber. Neretta's mouth hangs open and her eyes look as if they're about to start from her head.

"Do you hear me, gods? Do you hear me, seers?" Yaddair cries above the tumult. "The boy is not my son." When everyone is still, Yaddair explains, although he looks sorry to do so. "Gilan came to me almost two cycles ago from another settlement, telling me that she was with child. She said she had been raped and was begging for help. But the law that she would be stoned was unalterable, so to save her I wed her and brought her into my house. I have never once — not once — touched her. I've never had any inclination to do so. And I've never told anyone her story, not even First Wife. Had Morlova left well enough alone, or come to me quietly, nothing would ever have needed to be revealed."

"Why would she come to *you*?" sneers Morlova.

"Because I am Chief Seer of Vor and she trusted me, as she'd heard I was a kind man. And because she hoped I could change the law. And because, having been turned away by all the settlements between her community and ours, she had nowhere else to go."

Morlova drags Gilan up by the hair. "Is this true?" he yells. "Is it true?"

"Yes," she whispers. "Yes, may the gods help me, it is true. Yaddair, why have you divulged my shame?"

"To save my family. And you. You are safe now, protected by me, for I am still, and will remain, the Chief Seer of Vor."

Gilan's shame exposed to all, and his case in ruins, Morlova lets her fall, making a strange snorting noise as he does so. I thrust Miko into Neretta's arms and run to comfort Gilan. At the same time, the snow gathers force, pelting down heavy and thick.

"We should move somewhere less wet," Yaddair suggests, "into one of the antechambers, perhaps, although the tradition is that we gather here in Farlis and Solar. I'm sure that the seers of old who began the practice never experienced such miserable weather at this point in the cycle. Each cycle, the weather grows colder, until now it seems that Icer is, bit by bit, replacing Farlis. Come, I will order food and guren ale for all. That will warm us up."

Neretta stays where she is, looking as though she doesn't know whether to smile or frown, to laugh or scream at him. In the end she screams. "What you put me through, old man. What you put me through."

"I cannot trust your mouth, old woman," he replies quietly, "or I would have told you long ago. Don't make a spectacle of yourself in Council."

Neretta jiggles Miko angrily, but pauses before responding. She stares upwards. A shadow is falling over the chamber and she has seen what is to come. She shrieks as, together with the sheeting snow, darksome creatures begin to drop among us out of the gloomy skies. Their rags streaming behind them, they resemble big black swoopers, which hide in the lofts of dwellers, long fingers webbed into sharply pointed wings. As the creatures crash into the seers and fall to ground, they roll over, howling and groaning. Inside my head, I hear the words *"death, death, death."* Are these my thoughts, or theirs? And might they be vowing to kill us, or simply feeling their own deaths coming fast upon them?

Gilan scrambles up, hoists her long skirts above her knees, and bolts, paying no heed to Miko, who is screaming louder than Neretta. I have never seen Second Wife move so fast. "Oscurans," someone shouts, a nightmarish warning, as we all race from the Council House.

CHAPTER TEN

The seers escape the chamber faster than water floods out of an upturned pail. Most vanish towards their dwellings, no doubt to tell their families of the horrific occurrence, to tell their wives — with the children out of the room — that the Oscurans crashed into us as they fell. Others make for the smokies to pray to a god they believe lives in them. We've caught up with Gilan. Only she, Neretta, Miko, and I remain, shivering outside in the snow. The seers have all vanished. Neretta and I huddle together, sheltering Miko from the hail, which has now begun to fall. We are so close I can see the reflection of my terrified eyes in Neretta's. Our in-breathing is painful, out-breathing a freezing fog.

We have fled to what we hope is a safe distance from the ghastly creatures, have taken refuge under a zigzag tree, having slid and tripped in our haste to reach it. *Get lost*, it shouts at me. *This is my space*. It shoves me with a twiggy arm. I shove it back.

"At least the old man is still Chief Seer. But where is he?" asks Neretta, looking around. "I thought he would follow us."

I'm frightened to think what might have happened to him.

We wait, but he doesn't come. Weak with fear, I slip from Neretta and sink to the ground. She helps me back up with one hand, holding Miko fast with the other. Gilan is standing apart from us, glaring at Edge. She says nothing. Impossible, as usual, to know what she's thinking, but she doesn't look friendly.

"My nightmare has come true," I groan. "One way or another, those *things* will kill us."

"You must go and find Yaddair," Neretta screeches at me. "Before we freeze or are attacked by those … those … monsters. I cannot go, as I have to look after the children." She means Miko, of course. It takes me a moment to realize she is also speaking of Gilan, who is a little older than I am. "Remind him we dressed for Farlis and are dying of cold and fright, and if he doesn't return this instant, we will make our own way back to the castrel, lock the door against him, and close the shutters."

Miko grabs her hand, pulls two of her fingers into his mouth, and sucks. She lifts a corner of her robes, folding him into it. Unable to move, he begins to bawl again. "Go and find Yaddair," she repeats, distraught.

"You mean, go back inside?" I can't believe she would send me.

"Yes, you must. Where else could he be?" Her voice breaks and she begins to cry along with Miko. "Perhaps the old man is dead."

"No. He's alive. I feel it." My teeth chatter. My legs quake. But I must go back, because she's afraid to, and because, as I now realize, in her own strange way she actually loves him. Although I'm deathly afraid too, I must push myself to do it because I feel sorry for her. Also because I'm *baseborn* and need to do as I'm told.

Our footprints leading to this tree are already erased. A branch, drifted up with snow, cracks nearby, and I lurch forward as it showers ice on me. Gilan races away in the direction of the castrel, the falling hail glittering like her gauzy blood. Sure that the world I'm familiar with is ending, I drag myself into the Council House.

Yaddair is standing in the Council Chamber. There are scattered pools of darkness, shadowed tangles of what look like wings, legs, and rags lying half covered in snow, but the moaning has ceased. The voice in my head has gone quiet, too.

"You have nothing to fear, Arien," Yaddair says. "Nor, any longer, have they." He turns one of the creatures over with his foot. I jump back. Its body, which looks burned, is partly transparent and its eyes have retreated into its head. It is even more horrific than in my dreams.

"They are dead," Yaddair says. "Quite dead. I spoke to one of them, but it seemed he couldn't understand Kondaran. In any case, it was too late. His body twisted and he died."

So it must have been the Oscuran speaking to me, and me only, reporting his own impending death. I don't breathe a word of this to Yaddair. Mother used to tell Father that hearing speech that no one else could hear was unnatural, a curse rather than a gift. If it ever happened to her, she said, she would block her ears and set her mind against it. That's all very well, but those who speak or sing inside my mind don't seem to need permission, and I have no filter that could shut them out. It must have been the same for Father.

"Come, let us leave this place." Yaddair takes my arm. "We will bury them in due course."

I half expect them to disappear, perhaps in a flash of fire, but they don't, although they appear to be fraying at the edges. The danger, in any event, seems to be over, at least for the moment, but there is a stink of rotten fish. "I think they must have been fishermen," I say later, when Yaddair and Neretta are sitting by the hearth watching the fire, their faces flushed with heat. Neretta invites me to join them and share supper. For the first time in the castrel I feel accepted, as if I belong to the family.

"Yes," Yaddair agrees. "They likely bored holes in the thick ice of their sunless world. They had to eat something, after all, and crops — at least the ones I know of — don't do well in the dark. Perhaps they also stole from our barns and granaries while we slept and the sun was so low in the sky that they didn't find the heat unbearable. That would explain the missing grains that you're always complaining of, Old Woman. I must admit I didn't pay you much heed. I'm sorry for that."

"I always believed the tales that there were creatures on the other side of Edge, but never imagined they might have wings," she says. "They flew among us, dived into our lives. I hope never to see their like again. I'm afraid for the children, Miko as well. He's more my child than Gilan's."

"The creatures were so thin and so translucent. In the parts of them that weren't burned I could see their bones through the skin." I shudder. "Their wings were sharp and serrated as cookroom knives."

"They are gone now," says Yaddair. "Some of the dwellers in my employ buried them on the line between Vor and Edge, though the men said that there wasn't much to bury, and the earth was still hard from Icer. The creatures were beginning to disintegrate in our warmer air. It would be impossible for them to stay here long without dying, so we don't need to worry about the possibility of their staging a battle against us. They appeared starving. Or sick. Or both. May the gods protect their souls — if they have them."

Neretta makes the prayer sign, the first time I've ever seen her do so. Although I resist praying, I'm still afraid the Oscurans will continue to haunt Vor. It's so near Edge that our settlement would be their most likely route in.

Yaddair says, perhaps to soothe us, that no more of the creatures will come. But almost immediately something much worse happens. The earth begins to sway and heave; we're thrown across the cookroom wall with the furniture, can hear the twins and Miko screaming above the rumbling. Neretta rushes to see if the children are hurt. Yaddair runs to the window. "It's neither of our smokies. All is calm with them."

"It's the Cauldron," I say in terror. "It has erupted. My friend Radol once said that if it did we would feel it everywhere on Kondar. May the gods save him and his parents." I make the prayer sign — I have resisted it for so long — just as Neretta did. I picture Radol dead. I wonder how two appalling tragedies can happen at the same time. I cannot remove my hands from my face, for if I do, Yaddair will see that I'm crying.

* * *

Days later, still grieving, I dream of Radol. We walk in the swift beasts' pasture together. I pat one of the beasts, pick the flowers that fleck the landscape and wind them around one of its two tails. Skytrees from my old home bend in the breeze, singing. Radol lifts me high to pick a lush fruit. I feed it to the swift beast and it groans with pleasure. It is only when I feel happy and secure that the ground turns to jelly and Oscurans fly overhead, their rags strung out behind them. *"Death, death, death,"* they cry, and *"help us, aid us, save us,"* before vanishing in a fog of smoke.

Radol vanishes too. Lightside goes dark. I count one yellow and two green crescents and a myriad of tiny spangles. Though I've never seen anything like them before, I know them from my studies to be moons and stars. I'm now sure that I must be dreaming, as my teacher said two moons only cross the heavens above Kondar. The dream breaks open suddenly, like an egg cracking, and I'm awake. There's a strange keening noise. Peering out the window, I watch in horror as swooper-like creatures stream by, slicing the sky like knives before falling to ground. *We are sick unto death,* a voice in my head whispers. *Though we came to Vor to escape the pestilence in our dark place, it is too late. We are dying.*

I do not know why the creature has chosen to speak to me. I don't want his words or his sorrow and try to push them away. I have no idea what a pestilence is, but it sounds dreadful. And truth be told, I have enough sorrows of my own without him adding to them.

CHAPTER ELEVEN

The Oscurans continue to swoop over the landscape for two more days. They drop like dead flutterers onto the hills, onto the wold, pastures, and dwellings. One hits a burden beast, remains draped across it as the poor creature tries to shake it off. Two fall through our roof, destroying parts of it, and die quite horrifically on the floor of an upstairs hallway. Yaddair goes to find men to bury them, but the community is in such disarray from both the Cauldron and Oscurans he can find no one to do the work. He soon returns and asks my help.

"Don't touch them," he warns. "Wear your hand warmers."

I'm relieved to be busy, however upsetting the task, and am reminded of my mother, always working, always trying to avoid her distressing thoughts. Yaddair and I drag the ugly things downstairs and outside, and Yaddair hands me a small spade from the barn, keeping a bigger one for himself. After digging a shallow trench, we push the creatures in with our feet. They turn over and over, cleaving to one another as if still alive. As we start to throw earth on them I hear the remnant of a voice in my head but can't decipher what it's saying. One of the dead Oscurans is still trying to mind-speak. Or perhaps it's Radol, trying to reach me from the grave, where he most surely must be. I begin to cry. I see tears in Yaddair's eyes too, but they must be for a different reason. He's seeing his world — which must always have appeared so stable — disintegrate.

He returns to the settlement the next day, taking me with him, hoping to find someone who can fix the roof before it rains. "The quaking of the earth has stopped, and the Oscurans that fall are quickly locked in the cold ground forever," he says to anyone who is still sane enough to listen. "They are no threat to us. Are they?" he asks me pointedly, and I realize he has brought me along simply to confirm what he says.

"No," I reply obediently, "they are not." But the situation is not ameliorating. It is becoming much worse. Despite what Yaddair has said, grotesque bodies, half dissolved, remain in the wold and pastures, as more plummet to earth. The ground itself continues to rumble, and there are several tremors. Dwellers run from home to home, screaming with fear at the least sound or movement of the earth. I want to scream too, though I've managed to stop my mouth at the castrel for the sake of the children. But my loss is different from the losses of others. My loss — of Radol, that is — is personal and profound.

Yaddair says he's never seen anything like what's happening in the settlement, not even in the battles of his youth. But then, as suddenly as it began, the onslaught from Oscura stops. Not a single loathsome creature flies in front of the sun or litters Vor for days. I no longer hear their frantic voices. I concentrate instead on my almost certain loss of my oldest and dearest friend.

Slowly, as the weather warms, the community returns to normal. Or rather, to a new normal. Remnants of the Oscurans and their rags are buried close to Edge. The earth, after one last shudder, finally stills. Yaddair visits the dwellers again to encourage them back to their labour. "No one, Vorian dwellers," he says, "was killed or even injured, and the problem has been dealt with by my constant prayers to the gods."

He sends the other seers out too. "Find and feed your beasts," they say. The beasts, untended, have been roaming all over Seersland and the rest of Vor. "Plant your crops as fast as you can, or there will be nothing to gather come harvestime."

As if sleepwalking, still dazed with shock, most of the dwellers comply, strewing the seeds in furrows. They tie their children to them for fear they'll run off or get taken. I place the end of a thin leather cord around Miko's waist as I work, and attach the other end to my belt, as I've seen the dwellers do. Still scared, I watch the sky for dark shadows and listen for more smokie rumblings; I want the baby close to me in case something else untoward happens. The girls are too old to tie up, but I do my best to ensure that when they're with me they stay within shouting distance.

"Yanna, Beklee," I call one day, my heart pounding when I can't find them.

"We're here, Arien," they call back. "We were just hiding behind a tree in case the black things fall on us out of the sky."

"I wouldn't let them harm you. I would be your shield. Stay where I can see you."

They giggle and run from tree to tree as if we're playing hide-and-find. Although exhausted, I tie Miko's cord to a low branch and run to catch them. I want to slap both of them, but restrain myself, yelling at them instead. They look at me in astonishment.

There is still worry in the settlement. No, worry is too weak a word. There is fear: a constant peering at the heavens, a trembling of the hands, perhaps a tightness in the chest. A few dwellers are so frightened that they don't come to the wold at all. They remain locked in their dwellings until hunger or loneliness forces them out.

One day, while planting, I straighten to ease my back and notice two tall men standing against the horizon. Although they look familiar, I can't recall where I might have seen them before. One appears to be writing on a strange tablet without a stylus. They do not approach but before going on their way watch the dwellers, me included, covering seeds with earth. I feel prickles along my spine as I tell Neretta about them. She shrugs. "Just visitors," she says, as she turns a lump of dough on the table and pummels it with her knuckles. "Travel-bys, who come here by accident or on their way elsewhere." With her floury hand she brushes aside a lock of greyish brown hair that has fallen over her eyes, her round face placid for once.

I think she might be wrong about the strangers. They are too tall, too pale, too golden-eyed to be taken for casual travel-bys. And I can place them now. They were present when I was taken from my home in Katannya. I'm cautious about labelling them but feel they're followers, perhaps observers. They are the watchers, as I begin to call them. They watch where there is or has been trouble, and just possibly where something else unfortunate is about to take place. The unsettling thing is that they seem to be watching *me*. This last thought disturbs me greatly, causing me many sleepless nights. But since I don't know for sure who or why they watch, or even if they really do, I take care not to disagree with Neretta.

A young boy, one of Yaddair's workers, is at the cookroom door, breathless and dishevelled. "Please tell Chief Seer that Dweller Furna says that all the drogs in the barn are dead or dying, and could he come quick?"

Dismayed, I run to fetch Yaddair. I'm upset when any kindly beast suffers or dies, though I'm not the sort to fawn over drogs like an old woman, except when one is newborn, tiny and helpless. My heart melts as its little pink belly heaves up and down while it feeds. I even adopted a runt once. She was starving, as all her larger siblings crowded her out when she tried to approach her mother. She was so small I could hold her in the palm of one hand and feel her tiny heart beating furiously. I fed her at first by letting her lick milk from my finger and taught her tricks as she grew bigger. I gave her away at Mother's insistence when she was full grown and healthy. A farmer in need of a drog to corral his wool beasts took her. I cried for days, but was sometimes able to visit her, or watch her working in the wold. That drog of mine lived well into old age, unlike Yaddair's drogs, who have been struck down for no reason I can imagine.

Yaddair is baffled too. "What have you been feeding them?" he asks the boy, when he returns with me from the backroom, where I imagine he's been studying the secrets of the seers. His words are sharp-edged.

"The usual stuff, Chief Seer. Just dried grunt meat, pieces of salted milk beast, and grain. And the occasional piece of raw purple root as a treat."

"Nothing else? You're sure? They didn't get hold of some of those warty toad berries or the like?"

"No, Chief Seer. Them berries don't come ripe till late Solar. Furna told me most particular to say so, and also tell you that two of them were throwing up yesterday after they'd had a short run in the wold near Edge."

"That's odd."

"Afterwards they wouldn't eat nothing, couldn't even keep water down. This morn he found them dying, not just them two but all the others as well, when he came to feed them. I love them drogs …"

"Yes, yes." Yaddair sounds impatient. "I'm sure you do."

"It is the most pathetical sight you could ever see, Chief Seer. Blood everywhere." The boy sniffs and wipes his nose on his sleeve.

"Blood, you say? That's even odder. Perhaps a death dragon got to them. I'll come at once."

Neretta has his seer's cloak ready, and throws it over his shoulders as he vanishes through the door. "Not that it's a cold day, but with his stick it gives him an air of author-ity," she tells me. She's very sensitive to such matters since he almost lost his position to Morlova.

"The boy was right. Nothing to be done," Yaddair tells us when he returns. "They're all dead. The men will need to clean out the barn." He doesn't speak of his regret at the drogs' deaths, but his face looks older, frailer. It alarms me. "I'll buy some new drogs after a few days. We need them to guard the castrel and the wold from wild beasts. I cannot figure out what happened to them," he goes on. "I know of no illness like it in either man or beast. One moment they were healthy, the next crashing down and heaving blood from their nostrils and mouths. And after checking I realized there's no way a predator could get into that barn. Furna sleeps by the only door, which he locks every night." He disappears into the backroom. I imagine drogs, Oscurans, and Radol conflated behind my closed eyes.

Three days later, Furna is dead too. He lies in a pool of blood. His family takes him down the hill to the settlement, keening, shouting their grief. "But," says Neretta, "he was getting on in cycles. Perhaps the loss of the drogs was too much for him."

Soon after, to our shocked surprise, Morlova pushes the door open and strides into the cookroom. I draw back.

"Yaddair isn't here. Get out," Neretta says without ceremony. She swivels on her chair until her back is to him.

"Don't fret," he says. "I come in peace."

"That's kind of you." Neretta's words are icy with sarcasm. She swivels back. Sitting at the table sewing, she twists her face into a malevolent scowl and makes no effort to rise.

Her rudeness is obvious, but Morlova, undeterred, continues. "Dear lady, even though you may still be angry at what happened, something I blame myself for entirely, I must tell you that drogs everywhere in Vor are dying, but more important, a young man in the settlement, Anar, is now very ill. He has strange symptoms that the women don't know how to treat. Though they've tried every remedy they know, nothing works."

"A sick boy, you say? I'm not surprised. There've been all manner of mysterious doings around here lately too. And the dweller women are not in the least expert at healing anything, not even a cat."

"That's why I'm here. This morning I was told by one of the wives that you grow special restorative plants and mix your own medicines for the unwell, so I came — no, ran — to the castrel, hoping against hope for your assistance." He bows to Neretta before saying pitifully, "I don't know what else to do. The boy, Anar, is my nephew."

"Has he fever?" she asks. "Which type of ague does he suffer from, the hot or the cold?" She doesn't wait for an answer but stands up from the table, empties her basket of the remainder of last Solar's apple-fruits, and bustles around the cookroom tossing sundry items into it. In go a knife and a spool of ducan thread.

"He's as hot as fire, but will not drink, not a single drop. He says that water tastes of blood. His mother, my sister, is beside herself with worry."

Two small bunches of herbs and a clay bottle disappear into the basket. "I know where Anar and his mother live. Go now, while I finish gathering up my herbs and lotions. Uncover him, even if his mother protests. Since it sounds like a hot ague, be sure to put cold damp clouts on his face and body."

"Clouts?" asks Morlova.

"Cloths, rags, anything fabric you can find."

He swallows. "Thank you, First Wife. I am indebted to you."

"Yes, you are," Neretta says bluntly. "I want to be clear that I don't come for your sake, but for the sake of the boy."

"Thank you, First Wife," Morlova says again. "I understand." He actually bows.

"I'll be there presently, and do my best to help, but only the gods can save him, and only if they have the will to do so."

"I understand." Morlova repeats, before he vanishes through the door. I hear him rushing down the path towards the dwellings. The drogs hated him, and used to howl whenever he was near, but they are gone now, every one of them, and only silence greets his footsteps. Neretta assigns me the task of making a poultice from the cooked gulrid grain left over from breakfast; she shows me how to mix the cold grain with flutterer fat and encase it in one of the largest squares of material she keeps in the store room. She tells me to dampen the package with a ladle of water.

"It would be well if you came with me, Arien," she says. "I would be grateful for your help, and at the same time you could learn some of my secrets." She yells up the stairs, "Rouse yourself, Gilan, and do something useful for once. I entrust all three children to your care. Make sure they're fit and fed when Arien and I return."

There is not even the hint of a reply, so Neretta sticks her head around the door to tell Beklee and Yanna, who are playing patter ball against the castrel wall, to look after Miko when he wakes up. "And don't you girls go breaking any windows with that ball."

"Of course not," answers Yanna.

"D'you think we're babies?" asks Beklee.

"Should we wear hand warmers," I ask Neretta before we leave, "though the day is already growing hot? Your husband believes them protective." I already have mine, hidden in a pouch under my tunic. They cause a slight bulge in the fabric. It doesn't matter. Even in Solar, I take them with me everywhere. There's no knowing when or if we'll get another downpour of death-bound Oscurans.

"Stupid old man. What does he know?" But Neretta digs her own hand warmers out of what she calls her copburde, which contains her Icer clothing. She places the warmers in her basket. "Although I'm sure he's wrong," she tells me, "every now and then it turns out that he's right."

CHAPTER TWELVE

Anar appears to be very sick, apparently after ploughing the wold near Edge.

"The drog he took with him," says his mother, "is very poorly too."

"Did he come across anything unusual while he was turning the earth?" I ask his mother.

"What looked like black rags, he said. And bone fragments thin as needles."

He'd found the remains of the Oscurans. Dead though they were, they must have infected him and the drog. Although I feel it may be hopeless, we do everything possible for him. First we rip his quilt off, for his mother fought with Morlova earlier as he attempted to do so. She screams that we must put it back, that the lack of heat will kill him.

"It's a warm day," says Neretta, "and he's hotter still. We must cool, not warm him."

She continues to scream. Morlova drags his sister outside, gripping her arms so she can't escape, as we wash Anar all over with tepid water, leaving cool wet cloths on his arms and legs to quell the fever. Later we turn him onto his belly. Angry blue-grey boils have appeared on his back.

"I've never seen their like," says Neretta. "I'm baffled." After peering at the boils a second time, she calls for the poultice. As we apply it, praying to the gods to cure him, the boils begin to fester and spread. Neretta softens nartle and janny herbs in warm water. "They are best for fever," she tells me. She adds maymint, explaining that it's good for eruptions of the skin, and strains the mixture through a sieve that I find in the cookroom.

"Should we lance the boils with your knife?" I ask.

"I wondered about that. It's the usual remedy, but I'm afraid it might kill him straight away if we do."

Lacking any other ideas we turn him back over and prop him up. I hold his lips apart while she spoons small amounts of remedy into him. She massages his throat so he swallows.

He opens his eyes briefly, and I smile at him, thinking the disease, whatever it might be, is waning. I hasten outside to try to help the drog. But it's already dead.

When I return, Anar's eyes are closed again. We try to feed him more remedy, but he starts making a rattling sound as his gold-red blood leaks out of his mouth and onto the floor. Nothing we try helps. He never reopens his eyes. By evening, despite our best efforts, he is dead. We take off our sopping hand warmers and put them in the basket. When we tell her the tragic news, his mother screeches that we have murdered him. I already feel miserable and guilty. Her shrieking gives me a dreadful headache, as though someone is wringing out my brain like a piece of wet washing.

"We did everything we could," Neretta replies quietly. "We were called in too late. He was all skin and bones, poor boy. And he had symptoms the like of which I've never seen."

"He was strong and healthy two days ago. You killed him, I say."

"Hush," Morlova tells her. "They laboured all day to save the boy. And the girl tried to help the drog. But ultimately it was in the hands of the gods."

"You ... you ... *monsters*, you murdered him," she shouts again. My heart throbs with self-doubt and pity.

As we walk home, Neretta is pensive, her eyes downcast. I'm almost sure she's thinking of her girls, of how quickly their lives could be snuffed out.

Morlova runs after us to thank us for our efforts.

"We did our best to save him, as you told his mother, but our best wasn't good enough," Neretta says simply. "I'm sorry." With this short apology, all wounds between them appear salved.

Morlova touches her hand briefly and bows before returning to comfort his sister. As we approach the castrel, and I catch sight of blue and yellow flowers releasing their downy seeds across the wold, my eyes blur. Radol, who is always close by, at least in my thoughts, was of an age with Anar when we were forced apart. Now, more than likely, he's been crushed — turned to stone — by an eruption of the Cauldron. I cry bitterly, both for him and for myself. Neretta hugs me, mistaking the reason for my tears. "We will speak to Yaddair," she says. "Perhaps he will find a way to stop this scourge that is upon us."

"First the Oscurans, then our drogs and others in the settlement, now Anar, nephew of Morlova," she says to

Yaddair, late in the evening, after she has recounted the whole story.

"Anar was digging near where the men buried the Oscurans," I say. "Our drogs were in the same area just before they died. That must have something to do with it. Or perhaps the darksiders passed their sickness on when they fell among us."

"We can only wait. Time will tell," Yaddair replies, his voice low.

"Who's next?" Neretta asks him.

"We shall see. I hope no one. In the meantime we must tell the dwellers to avoid the area of the burial place, and make sure their beasts do too. I would give orders to dig the remains up and burn them, but I fear that might make the situation worse." He is Chief Seer of Vor. It is his job to interpret the will of the gods. But I can see by his haunted eyes that like me he believes it too late, that the gods, if gods there be, have abandoned us.

CHAPTER THIRTEEN

On an unusually fine day during early Solar, when the sun is shining strong and bright, the trees are fully leafed, and there's not so much as a cloud or wisp of fog in the sky, two of the dwellers who have been celebrating Varkinalia — the coming of the heat and the ripening of the grain — with guren ale, fresh sweet bread, and dances to the gods, fall down in a narrow pathway of the settlement. At first others believe them drunk, and shake them in an attempt to make them pull themselves together and go home. But there's no response. The dwellers are unconscious. Soon another man drops. Then a woman.

How do I know all this? A dweller just rushed up to the castrel to report what's happening, telling us that those still well are shrieking and tearing out their hair.

Neretta and I hurry down to the settlement to do what we can for the sick, but three of the four die anyway. Our herbs and poultices are useless. I throw a handful of janny herbs and nartle leaves into the air. They drift down like snow.

Within hours we are at the beginning of what Yaddair calls a plague. Many are trying to escape Vor. Fear of disease and the condition of those suffering at first haunt me too, but as the numbers of sick and dead increase I still push myself to go out daily, in part to avoid thinking. As we go, I hold Neretta's basket of remedies — which we are constantly remixing to find a cure — and apply cold poultices of mud mixed with water to those who fall along the pathways and in the dwellings of Vor. We can't keep using grain and flutterer fat. We'll run out of food if we do.

I become so used to the habit of nursing with her, tending to ravaged bodies, wiping fevered brows, that eventually I hardly notice the horrific condition and distress of the dying. Shameful as it is to admit, I have grown numb to their suffering. It's the only way I can cope. They are simply the clay that I work with, whether my efforts are successful or not. At the moment, for the most part, they're not.

Yaddair has appeared in the settlement too, counselling the sick and their families. Appalled — as he tells us — by the bodies left festering in the streets, he tries to find dwellers who aren't afraid to carry the dead away and bury them. After exchanging his seer's robes for the coarse clothing worn by wold labourers, he starts to entomb in earth — with the few dwellers brave enough to aid him — those who have perished. He begs the gods for an end to the blight as he digs. Most of the other seers have fled or stay locked in their dwellings. But, old enmities forgotten since the death of his nephew, Morlova hastens to help Yaddair comfort the bereaved and scoop out trenches in which to throw the bodies. Days later, the two seers confer in the backroom of the castrel about what should be done next.

Neretta and I hear the odd word as I wash Miko before bed. The girls sluice themselves down, scarcely dirty as Neretta has forbidden them to play outside. She locks the children, protesting, in the castrel when we go to attend to the sick. When we return, we remove our hand warmers and wash our hands thoroughly before touching them, so as not to pass on any trace of the sickness that may be lingering on our fingers.

The words we overhear through the door aren't pleasant: managing, containing, disposing, and "Edge-dwellers' plague," as it's come to be called, though the creatures almost certainly come from beyond Edge. It's an imprecise term, much as my label of baseborn is. The voices of the two seers rise and fall. Occasionally, when they aren't in agreement, there's the clanging sound of argument, but we're not sure what it's about. Gilan's usual loud sobbing upstairs masks most of the details of their conversation. They emerge from the backroom, finalizing plans, as we're drying the children. The girls blush at the appearance of a virtual stranger, hastily girding themselves in the last of our towels before running away to their room and dressing before returning.

"Morlova," says Yaddair, "as we discussed, you are to go to Braban right away to see the Chief Seer there. I will go down to the settlement to ask the dwellers and seers — those who are left — to meet us without fail in the wold close to Bachen Stream. We will speak to them there."

"The Council Chamber would be better," says Morlova. "It, too, is open to the fresh air, which might be curative. And it will give our plans the aura of authority."

"Council Chamber it is," agrees Yaddair, "and no more arguing about our strategies or anything else, if we can manage it. We need to be strong and united; we need to set an example to the dwellers."

"I was mistaken about you. You're a good man," Morlova says.

"As are you," replies Yaddair. They clasp each other's hands before Morlova flies out the door, presumably on his way to Braban.

"Wonders will never cease. I was always concerned that they would end up breaking each other's heads. Now they're thick as thieves. What do you think this is about?" Neretta asks me in a whisper as Morlova leaves. Of course I have no idea. "It's a puzzle and no mistake," she says. "I will attend the meeting also," she tells Yaddair, "to hear what's to be heard and do what's to be done. And Arien, if she wishes, may accompany me."

"I would very much like to go," I say.

"You are both to stay home. As it is, you put yourselves in danger every day. I will explain to you later what we're planning."

"We shall go," insists Neretta. "You constantly put yourself in danger too, old man, and it's our job, thankless though it may be, to stand by you. It's a mercy, though, and perhaps a sign from the gods, that not one of us here has fallen prey to the sickness."

"So far." Yaddair knits his brows as if about to chastise her, but instead thrusts his head forward, thin lips set in a grim line. "Very well, old woman. On the morrow you can both come hear the rules that Morlova and I will impose on the dwellers — and for the most part, on ourselves."

"I'll finish making supper now," Neretta decides. "Girls, Miko, off to bed with you."

She turns to Yaddair when they've gone. "What can we do? The children, even if they stay indoors, are in the gravest danger. Every day our clothes reek of the dead and diseased when we return from the settlement. I couldn't bear for any of them to succumb." She doesn't differentiate between the girls and Miko any longer, has come to accept him as her own child.

"I will think on it, old woman. We will find a way to protect them from the Edge-dwellers' plague, never fear."

"I do fear. And I won't stop fearing till they're safe."

Later I go to check on the children. Miko, who now shares a room with his pretend sisters, is asleep in his small bed. He's lying on his back, his arms flung wide. Yanna and Beklee are curled up on sleep-mats with their quilts drawn over their heads — for comfort, I imagine. Unlike me, they seem not to fear the dark; however, I do remember pulling my coverings up as far as my nose — but no higher — when I was younger and felt threatened or afraid. The girls are whispering to each other through their quilts, of an age now to understand at least something of what's happening. I'd like to hug them but don't wish to disturb their sister talk. They are concerned about tomorrow. I'm concerned too. What is Yaddair about to tell us all? I creep out of their room and away from the castrel to pick, in solitude and cooler air, more herbs for Neretta's useless remedies.

CHAPTER FOURTEEN

Yaddair stands on a dais of rock in the Council Chamber dressed in his purple cassock, his stave in hand. There is a whirring sound, barely noticeable over the murmurs of conversation, as the eye opens and glares at the gathering. Many are chastened by the baleful stare and lapse into silence. Morlova stands next to Yaddair, also in full regalia. Both wear amulets on heavy metal chains; Yaddair's is fashioned in silver and has a somewhat more ornate appearance than Morlova's, signalling that he is in charge of the proceedings. He quickly presents his credentials: "Dwellers, I have been your Chief Seer since the ruinous cycle when the rivers rose up and covered the lower wolds of Seersland and many of the dwellings of Vor. After consulting with the gods, I entreated the waters to recede, and they did, saving many lives."

Some of the older dwellers nod their heads, remembering.

"I care for your welfare as much now as I did then. This is my present wish: That you stand as far apart as possible, so that no one passes sickness to anybody else."

A shuffling sound can be heard as the dwellers rearrange themselves. After moving as far from one another as possible, they gaze around the Council Chamber, a place they've no doubt imagined all their lives but been forbidden to enter, as it's the secret and most private place of the seers. This is where they conduct their mysterious business with the gods. Perhaps the dwellers — as I did the first time I came here — expect extravagant paintings, complicated runes, and luxurious hangings on the walls. Perhaps they expect mystic arcs, undecipherable puzzles, and circles on the dais. There are no such decorations. The Council Chamber is a large plain room starkly panelled in mutetree wood. It is circular so that there are no corners for evil spirits to hide in. A breeze wafts around the chamber as there's no roof. After a moment, one of the dwellers is emboldened to speak.

"I heard tell that you two seers were quarrelling, not long since," he says.

"We are united in our obedience to the gods and our care for you, the dwellers of Vor," Morlova replies. "Now is not the time to bring up past discords. Now is the time to heal. We have made peace with each other and will work together for the greater good of the settlement."

"If you were as magical as seers are supposed to be, you would end this plague."

"We are merely the instruments of the gods," Yaddair responds. "We may suggest remedies for ills in the settlement, but ultimately we must obey the gods' instructions, and communicate to the dwellers their intentions. At this tragic time, we have been enlisted to report the following: The plague is sent to purify Vor and its people. Be comforted, for there is not one but several worlds after this one for those

who are righteous yet succumb to the pestilence, and they
are kinder worlds with no hunger or Icer."

"That's almost worth dying for." The lively looking fellow
who spoke before grins.

"Shh," say one or two others.

"Have respect, Ereni," calls out one of the women, "or
you won't get there." Even in the midst of our tragedy, there
is a trill of laughter from all around her.

Yaddair waits for the laughter to subside before raising
his stave high in the air. "The gods have decreed that no one
may leave the settlement, and that all of us in Vor must keep
ourselves to ourselves, separate from the rest of Kondar, to
avoid infecting other settlements. If one is sick in a dwelling,
the rest of the family must remain inside until all threat of
contagion has passed. For this … this *scourge* surely may be
passed from one to another."

A sigh rises from the dwellers. "But then we shall be
imprisoned," cries a young girl, "with those who have the
sickness. Like a scavenging wild-beast, it will kill us all."

"Before we could go out into the forests and hills to try to
escape it," whimpers a woman. "Now we are caught in its nets."

"You are most welcome to come into the forests and
wolds of Seersland whenever you wish to," says Yaddair.
"There is plenty of room to be alone in my wolds."

It's as if the woman hasn't heard him. "Now we have no
recourse but to stay and die. Our children will die too. My
sister's girl is already close to death."

"I will come and issue a blessing to her and her family.
Meanwhile, have faith," Morlova tells her. "Rejoice in the
gods and be obedient to their wills. Let us show our unself-
ishness. Without meaning to, the Oscurans visited their

sickness onto us. The gods say we can avoid doing the same to others by keeping our distance from them."

Yaddair speaks again. Doubtless he and Morlova rehearsed what they were going to say yesterday evening. Their object is selfless and praiseworthy, but intensely frightening to those in the chamber. Everyone who was horror-struck at the onset of the plague is now doubly so, I'm sure. Only the numbness that has recently overtaken me prevents me from feeling the same way. I feel remote, uncaring. Even my skin feels benumbed.

"We must build a fence around Seersland and the settlement, so that no healthy person may enter, and no one — whether he believes he's infected or not — may leave. The sick will be shut in their dwellings until they recover. Their relatives will remain with them. I will expect the men, and perhaps some of the women, to approach Seer Morlova after the meeting and agree to monitor the dwellings and to serve in the cutting of wood and erecting of high wooden fences around Vor. We will also need sentries to guard the gates, chosen from those who we know will take pains to execute the rules. We need others to help bury the dead — within the fences but far from the dwellings — to avoid further contagion."

A murmur ripples through the chamber, that there is, after all, no evading the will of the gods.

"We must do as we are told, and surely we will be saved," says a young boy.

"How will we get food?" asks another.

"We will maintain our work in the wolds until harvestime. What we cannot grow, we will buy," says Yaddair.

"How can we do that?" asks a woman. "Who would come close enough to sell us food?"

"I sent Seer Morlova to speak to the Chief Seer of Braban last evening. He is willing to have his dwellers leave what we need just outside the fences on the high and windy Banard Rock in return for quoinies we'll drop into the small dead pool at the top," says Yaddair. "Rinsing the coins in the pool will satisfy the Chief Seer of Braban that they are clean and free of disease. Morlova and I will drop the quoinies into the pool, and collect whatever is sent in return."

"I have next to no quoinies to bargain with," the woman cries.

"That isn't a problem. I will donate as many quoinies as are needed until the crisis is over. I will sell my seer's amulet if necessary. It is solid silver and worth a great deal."

"That sounds more than fair, Chief Seer Yaddair," she says, brightening.

"Fair and generous," adds a woman standing a little way off from her, who despite the gravity of the situation, arrived at the Council House in a yellow pointed hat with red feathers and mauve berries decorating its brim. "It's likely my last opportunity to get dressed up," I hear her tell those around her.

"But if the gods say there is a wonderful afterlife, where it's always Farlis or Solar," a man at the front demands, "why would they want us to wall ourselves in and drop money in the dead pool to avoid infecting others? How sensible is that?"

This question, which I find rather clever, appears to perplex both Yaddair and Morlova. It cannot be what they expected. It is a direct affront to their authority, and to the faith of Kondarans. Yaddair steps forward, as if to answer. Morlova stops him, whispering in his ear. As the two consult each other, a rumble of complaint rises in the chamber.

"Yes," shouts a man at the back. "Why *is* that? Why would the gods send us such confusing messages?"

"Expel that dweller," cries out the feather-berry woman, "for challenging the gods."

It is Neretta who shuts everyone up by stepping forward and climbing onto the dais. A woman on the dais? A woman speaking in open Council? The dwellers are aghast.

She makes no apology for her presence. "The ways of the gods are mysterious indeed," she begins, reminding me of my mother. "Fellow dwellers, death is no bad thing, as by dying we pass through the portals that lead to the homes of the gods, where a pleasant new life free of hunger and pain awaits us. But the symptoms of this ague are fearsome. They are a test of faith. Think of our children of Vor and what they may have to endure, as the dweller over there mentioned. Would you wish others, especially young ones, to have to go through the dreadful pains of the pestilence also? If we are strong in our conviction we can avoid hurting those in other settlements as well as limit the sickness in our own.

"The gods are our spiritual parents. They will guide us as they have in the past. They will help us find a remedy. And Seer Morlova and Chief Seer Yaddair will lead us along the right path. They have to endure all that we have to endure, and more, for they stand firm against the sickness; they are out and around the suffering every day. If they are not frightened to attend to the dying or to bury the dead, neither should we be. If they are not afraid to face death, neither should we be. We Vorians are known as people of strength and courage. With the help of the gods we will battle this evil plague and in the end we will win." She stops, face almost purple with exertion. I've no idea whether she believes what she's saying, but have never heard her speak so bravely or so well.

"First Wife of Seer Yaddair counsels us right," an elderly dweller acknowledges quietly. "Even if she *is* a woman." His words pass from one to another until the chamber is again abuzz with talk.

"Bless you all," says Yaddair, lifting his stave. "Be strong. Take courage. The gods walk beside us in our time of need. We must be willing to sacrifice ourselves for the benefit of those others, innocent all, who with us share the sun on the Lightside of Kondar. The gods will aid us, either in this life or the next. If we are not courageous, if we do not take strength from our faith, it is possible that all those on Kondar will perish from the plague of the Edge dwellers."

On the way home, Yaddair thanks Neretta. "For once, old woman, it was good to hear your chatter."

"Load of rubbish, old man," she says, trying unsuccessfully to hide her grin behind the plants she is picking to use in new potions. Her apple-round cheeks crinkle with mirth, rare to see in these sad times. I'm not sure what she means by "rubbish," whether she might be speaking of her own words or those of Yaddair, but I'm proud of her actions this day and will try to be more outspoken myself, baseborn though I'm still considered.

Vor is changing. Others may feel imprisoned by the soon to be erected fences, yet I am becoming freer. Most of the seers have vanished to save themselves, so I don't feel bound by the old laws or traditions any longer. Neither Yaddair nor Neretta binds me to those laws, which are as creaky as the eye in Yaddair's stave. They now treat me as an equal. From here on out I must fight like Neretta for what's worth fighting for. Neretta appears to have calmed the dwellers and enlisted their help, cleverly speaking as if one of them. By doing so, she has ensured that Yaddair and Morlova's plans for the settlement will be implemented. I smile back at her through her bouquet of untried remedies. Now that Radol is gone and I'm left without hope of ever having a husband or family, Neretta's calling will be my calling too. I must not hold back but battle for what's right. It may rescue me from despair.

CHAPTER FIFTEEN

Yaddair calls the entire family, including the children, to a meeting. Gilan, as usual, ignores the summons.

"Neretta" — this is the first time I've heard him call her that — "you asked me how we could keep the children safe, and I've thought of a plan. Gilan's parents want her back, and I am proposing that we send her and Miko to them, as long as they'll accept you, Arien, and our daughters also, until this pestilence wears itself out."

"I'm not going anywhere," retorts Neretta. "I want very much to send the girls, though it seems strange to me to do so."

"Why is it strange?" asks Yaddair.

"Because we are asking everyone else to sacrifice for the good of the community, while keeping our girls and Gilan, Miko, and even Arien safe. I feel guilty about it."

"Look, old woman, you asked me to find a way to keep the children free of the plague, didn't you? This is the only way I can, though I feel guilt worming its way through my skull as well. But I can't save everybody, the gods know. I have put enough hard work into the settlement to take something out when I wish to, and that something is to send you and the children away. As I said to you yesterday, the dwellers will have to obey the rules, and we will too, *for the most part.*"

"I suppose you're right. We can compromise. We will send Gilan, Arien, and the children out, but I most certainly will stay, to help you, and to tend to the sick."

"No, Mother, no," cries Beklee. "I don't want to go to a strange place without you."

"You must go, daughter, though I hate the thought of losing you, even for a moment. It won't all be strangers. Yanna and Arien will be with you."

I don't like the way this plan is unfolding. "Seer Yaddair, I feel guilty also. I've no right to freedom while others are imprisoned with the illness. I need to stay and help Neretta devise new remedies, remix old ones, and try to help the sick."

He shakes his head. "No, Arien. I have finally come to the conclusion that First Wife, obstinate as she is, must do that which she feels right. She is my partner and I have been wrong to ignore her needs and desires all these cycles. I can no longer find it in my heart to order her about or send her away against her will. But in the absence of your parents, I am responsible for you, and I take that responsibility seriously. I want you safe, and I also know that Second Wife is incapable of taking three children anywhere, even if it's only to the outhouse, so I'm putting you in charge of the expedition."

I feel a scowl forming between my eyebrows. Yaddair fetches his stave and turns the eye towards me. It scowls back at me, if one eye can be said to be scowling.

"That … that … *thing* doesn't deter me," I retort. "I know the eye on your stick is managed by trickery, not magic. I have heard its gears whirring, know you're moving it, so you can't use it to frighten me into complying with your wishes."

"These are not my wishes but my *orders*," he says.

But I can be as stubborn as he is. As a last resort I throw in mention of divine powers. "The gods have told me that to stay here and nurse the sick is my obligation and my calling." I suddenly feel like the old me, the me who used to argue with my mother, the me whose blood courses fast and ancient through my veins. My true self has been frightened into absence for too long.

"Why, Arien, you have grown bold since last we spoke. It is unwise to challenge a seer, especially if you're a woman." He gives a half smile as he places his stick in the corner. "As *Chief* Seer, I've communed with the gods too, and they've decreed that for the safety of Miko, Beklee, and Yanna, as well as for your own, you must take them to Gilan's family, not more than a day's trekken from here." I bite my lip before bowing my head in acquiescence. We understand each other pretty well. This has nothing to do with the gods, but with the fact that a Chief Seer trumps a baseborn any day. I say nothing more. But I have a plan.

Yaddair leads me into the backroom, draws a map, shows me how to read it, and offers me an old swift beast, no longer swift, which I can seat the children on when they tire of walking — or rather *dancing* — along the way. He also gives me twenty-eight quoinies, begging me to keep them in a pouch under my tunic. I have never seen such wealth. "The quoinies are yours. Saved from what I didn't have to

pay that scoundrel in Katannya for you. Go with the gods …
if there are gods. Never tell anyone that I've said that." His
words remind me of my own misgivings. He has the same
doubts as I do. We smirk at each other like co-conspirators.
As I leave the room, Yaddair warns, "Take care. Make sure
that you and the children keep to the path. There are many
hidden dangers along the way."

"I will keep to the path with the children, Seer Yaddair,
no matter how narrow or winding it might be. You may be
sure of that."

We have to hurry if we are to leave, as the high fence is
already half built. Once it's up there'll be guards at the gate
and no escape. We wait until the sawing and hammering
stop in the middle of the night before Yaddair departs to
retrieve the swift beast from the pasture. No one bothers to
tell Gilan of Yaddair's plan until the beast stands at the door.
That way we don't have to deal with her moaning and grip-
ing until the last possible moment.

When we finally inform her, she cries, "I won't go anywhere without my best clothing, my wall hangings, and my
green paint. Someone must pack them for me." She stares at
me. Obviously, I'm the one commanded to do her bidding.
"And by the way, I don't need nasty messy girls at my parents'
dwelling. I can't stand you, baseborn, and I really don't want
that snotty baby, though I suppose my mother will be happy
to rear him."

As she stands in the centre of the cookroom, screeching
between bites of a pear-fruit, I wonder how she can be so
beautiful on the outside and so ugly within. She's the shal-
lowest and laziest person I've ever had the misfortune to
meet. If this is what wealth does to one, I prefer to stay poor.

Her selfishness is unfathomable. How can she show Yaddair and Neretta no gratitude?

"How can you reject your own son?" I demand angrily.

"I never wanted to have him, and I can't stand the sight of him now."

"After all Yaddair's done for you, you pathetic do-nothing. After he saved you from certain death, brought you and your soon-to-be-born baby to the house, and made me treat you like royalty — though in reality you're a gutter-beast and worse than any baseborn — you repay us like this? With nothing but snivelling, more snivelling, snarling, and screaming. What a disgrace you are to your family." Neretta fetches the broom and sweeps Gilan outside with it, jabbing her in the back with the broom handle for good measure. During the commotion I slide a sharp cookroom knife from the table and stick it in my belt against all eventualities. One can never be too careful, as my mother used to say.

Gilan hurls the pear onto the ground on the way out. Miko picks it up and chews on it, dirt and all. I remove it and attach his cord to him. He cries for the fruit.

Still carping — although somewhat less shrilly — Gilan climbs onto the slow-swift beast meant for the children and remains there for the whole journey. She complains about its smell, and how it might rub off on her. She complains of the sharpness of its ribs against her legs, and against other places better left unmentioned. She complains about the heat. She complains that her brain aches from all the exertion. She complains she has no fashionable clothes with her. She complains that we'll never get where we're going.

"You certainly won't," I mutter, "if you keep this up."

"You shut your mouth, baseborn."

"You shut yours or I'll knock you off the steed."

She says no more. We are entering the woods. It's becoming more and more drear. Trees from both sides of the path close in on us, whispering nasty tree words to one another, shutting out the pallid sun. I try to see the sky between the thick, sawtoothed branches, but cannot, panic both at the loss of light and at the realization we are on the verge of a killtree forest. It's so dark, I feel faint. Suddenly Miko's cord — which he's been struggling against — breaks. He runs headlong into a thicket as if playing hide-and-find the way the twins do. Before I can get to him, plant tendrils and vines twine themselves around his little body, scoop him up, and begin to squeeze. I rush after him, pull the knife from my belt and reach up, cutting and hacking with all my strength to release him. I catch him as he drops, while smashing more vines and creepers as they coil around him again. Once he is free, they begin to attack me, spiralling up my legs. It's a repeat on land of what must have happened to my parents in Icer Lake. I want to howl at the memory but am stopped by the sight of the girls rushing forward to help.

"Get back," I yell. "Stay on the path." They freeze, calling to Miko and me all the while. I'm desperate. I don't want to die here; I don't want Miko to die. Slashing through the foraging suckers before they get a decent leghold and trampling them underfoot, I rush towards the girls, Miko under my arm. His feet dangle loose and catch on twigs and branches. A vine slithers across the earth, takes hold of his ankle, and pulls. I try to break it off but it unravels as we run, growing longer and thicker while continuing to tighten its grip. I'm terrified he'll never break free of it, but when I finally manage to get us out of the poisonous forest, leaping onto the path as if pursued by a three-cornered monster, it relinquishes its grip on him, retreating slowly into the stand of trees. My fear for his life has turned into fury. Instead of consoling him, I shake him and shout, "Don't you ever, ever, do that again. D'you hear?"

He nods dumbly, too afraid to cry.

"You naughty, naughty boy. I should smack you. You were about to be killed." I realize with a shock that I sound exactly like my mother. The dwellers have a saying: "All sons become their fathers." I'm not sure whether it's supposed to be a compliment or a criticism. But either way, they should probably add that all daughters end up like their mothers. I feel horribly guilty, give him a big hug and a few words of comfort before setting him down. Gilan, though, is another matter. Oblivious to her son's danger, she has trotted ahead. I want to drag her from the beast and pummel her.

There is one other incident. Two boys break out of a wood of zigzag trees and demand quoinies and jewels, saying that otherwise they'll throw us to the grinders in the pool nearby. It's likely they'll throw us in whether we meet their demands or not. I've often speculated that this is what happened to my parents at the hands of Farun, but I'll never be able to prove it. We've just made our way past the pool the boys speak of, in which fishy splashings can be heard. A large piece of ice in the centre looks like an upturned cooking pot. The water must still be freezing, but not too cold for grinders and spikels.

The girls scream and hug each other. Gilan draws her legs up so the boys can't reach her. She pulls on the reins hard to escape, but the beast appears to be an ambler.

Besides, it's not about to go anywhere, as it's found a tasty patch of meadow sweet, its seeds likely carried on the wind from some nearby farmer's wold. Miko doesn't notice what's happening. Crouched close to the ground, tied to me again on the repaired cord, he's busy playing with a wyrm, poking it and winding it around a little twig. Chortling, he appears to have forgotten his frightful experience with the killtrees earlier, which is just as well.

"We don't have any quoinies," I say calmly. The coins Yaddair gave me are tied in a pouch around my waist under my tunic. My heart is throbbing so hard I feel as if it's about to burst through the cage of my ribs. "And we certainly have no jewels, for what good is finery when we're dying?"

"Huh?"

"We're from the plague settlement of Vor. We have the Edge-dwellers' plague. If you touch us or we so much as breathe on you, bloody snakes will fly out of our mouths and bite you, so you will certainly succumb. We're about to die. Come any closer and the disease, if not my knife" — I flash it at them — "will slay you too."

In too much of a hurry to reply, they stumble over each other, vanishing like spirits into the woods. I tremble with relief. My blood is pumping loud and fast. For a moment I feel I can best anyone.

"Won't you be pleased to be home with your parents?" I say later to Gilan, trying, one last time, to strike up conversation.

"I suppose," she says grudgingly.

"We're almost there, according to Yaddair's map. You're so lucky. I can't imagine anything I'd like more than to be with my parents again in our little dwelling."

She turns her head away as if bored and clicks her tongue to urge the slow-swift beast on. I'm carrying Miko, who has fallen asleep, his curly head against my neck. I've been carrying him for at least half a day because he's so tired. His legs aren't long enough to keep pace with the bony beast, slow though it is. I'm exhausted too, and my arms ache. But I'm still moving. Once I slip off Miko's tether and try to sit him in front of Gilan but she pushes him off, and I just manage to catch him before he reaches the ground. Now he's awake and crying. I bundle him into my arms again. Until we reach Gilan's old dwelling, the girls and I have to stick together and stumble along the rocky paths beside Second Wife and her not-so-swift creature, or one or all of us may be prey to poison forests, thieves, or murderers.

CHAPTER SIXTEEN

After the girls and Miko have settled into their new home, I return with some trepidation to Vor. Who knows what might be waiting for me on the path? It's imperative I get back to the castrel though, to help Yaddair and Neretta battle the plague.

I sit high on my un-speedy beast as we amble along. I'm so exhausted I've decided we'll split the trip into two, finding a safe place to spend the night. There are no lurkers in the dark forests today, thieves or murderers, but all the same I feel a good deal safer when my feet aren't touching the ground. Just as well, as the second day we are overwhelmed halfway up a hill by an army of huge crawlers, fat and hairy, which scramble up my beast's legs. They chatter, chatter, chatter, and are beginning to spin webs around us. My teeth chatter too, as I bend down and try to push them off him. They are the size of huge water-fruits and utterly terrifying. My swift beast, startled, has for once been true to his name, and is galloping along as fast — perhaps not as the wind but as a stiff breeze. They begin to fall from him. His hooves trample them underfoot. His tails flare out behind him. One, and only one, manages to reach me, clambering up my hair to my head. I pull out my knife and hack off the strands to which the crawler clings. Embedded in the hair, it falls to the ground. The crawlers still alive screech even louder.

"Go away," I scream.

Chatter, chatter.

"For the love of the gods, what do you want with me?"

Chatter, chatter, chatter. Nice fresh meat, chatter, chatter — delicious.

Disgusted and terrified, I spur my beast up the hill. The crawlers finally drop off with some help from my luggers, but as we reach the crest something stirs lazily below us. Squinting at it, I realize immediately what it is: a death dragon. It lies right across the pathway that we have to cross to return to Vor. I've never seen one before and was not even sure they existed, though I've heard stories about them. But this one clearly does exist. My legs and arms prickle with fear at the sight of the thing. It's the size of my old dwelling, or even bigger. A huge green-bellied serpent, it's home to a nauseating knot of vermilion snakes that coil and stretch along its back. I hear them hissing, realize with absolute horror that they're part of the dragon. I see its monster fangs. I see its one eye. I imagine the power of its thick scaly tail, which is beginning to undulate towards me. Its tip reveals another head, which bares its own sharp fangs and spits at me. I smell smoke, see ribbons of fire.

The dragon's wings are folded below its glistening body. What if it suddenly takes flight? It would be on me in a flash. There'd be no time to flee. I've reached the poison forest, which lines both sides of the path, too dangerous to enter. If I go back I'll no doubt meet up with the giant crawlers again. We must somehow go forward. I halt my beast and stare at the dragon, quietly reaching under my tunic for my knife.

It stares back and mind-speaks at me, quite pathetically, in a deep raspy voice: *Nobody likes me and you don't either.*

How bizarre the monster is! However, I sense an opportunity to escape. "That's not true. I do like you, my beast likes you, and I know others who will absolutely adore you. Let me past and I'll go fetch them."

I have a hurt claw. Please, please, help me get up. I vow not to harm you. Dragons have codes of behaviour too, you know. It pulls one of its wings out from under it and begins to lick its webby folds, shedding purple dragon tears as it does so.

Wonder of wonders, my previously dumb beast is now mind-speaking — or rather mind-whispering so the dragon can't hear. *Mistress, I have a plan. Let me go forward.*

"It'll eat you."

Dragons, from what I've heard, don't like swift-beast flesh. I will wait on the other side of the monster while you pretend to help it up while slipping past. If it attacks you, take your knife and stab it in the eye. That's the only way to kill dragons, or so it's been said in the stables. I would stab it myself, but I can't hold a knife. I'll try to wound it from behind.

"I've never heard you mind-speak before."

I've never had anything important to say, nothing you couldn't deal with yourself. But now there's a great big something that will take the both of us to slay. I'll wait for you, never fear, and we'll canter all the way home. Be not afraid.

"I'll try not to be." I slide off him; he tiptoes — if swift beasts can be said to tiptoe — away from me and around the dragon, which doesn't touch him but sneers, as if loathing his warm yeasty smell. I hide my knife behind my back. "Let me help you up," I mind-say, approaching the monster cautiously, ready to rush past it.

Thank you, my dear. It is so kind of you. I have only one thing to tell you before we begin — in order that everything may proceed smoothly.

"And what is that?"

Never trust a dragon. I was too lazy to come to you, so you came to me. Now I have you.

Suddenly it rises. Its wings enfold and squeeze me. Its snakes hiss. Its tail's vicious mouth grabs my luggers and pulls. The luggers fall off. As I struggle against the dragon's massive strength, the tail writhes as it wraps itself tightly around me, singeing me with the flaming plumes that issue from its lips. It's strangling me, but, gasping for breath, I fight to get one hand free, the hand that's holding the knife. Finally I succeed. Feeling nothing but cold and consuming hatred, I stab the dragon's wings and tail over and over, till its grip loosens. As it bends its huge head to see what damage I've caused, I smash my blade into its single eye.

I plunge the knife deeply, once, twice, three times, until it's too deep to retrieve. Purple liquid gushes from its eye as I feel a series of violent shudders. At the same time, my swift beast is pounding the dragon's body from behind with all four of its hooves. Roaring in pain, the gigantic brute releases me, while the vermilion snakes slide from its back and begin to slither in my direction. Perhaps they too will grow into dragons, but this is no time to investigate their reproductive habits. The swift beast uses his hooves on them too, mashing a good number of them to pulp. My legs weak, I push through a gap between the wing and belly of the dragon to meet up with my heroic steed. He grabs my tunic with his soft mouth and swings me onto his back. *Here we go,* he laughs, triumphant. *I've not felt this strong in years.*

"From now on your name is Glory," I say, as we turn and gallop away towards Vor. I can't resist turning once more to the death dragon, which is screaming in agony, its death throes toppling the trees of the poison forest. "I have only one thing to say," I mind-tell it. "Never trust a baseborn."

CHAPTER SEVENTEEN

Unable to reach the castrel because of the newly erected fence, I ask the guard, through a grille, to open the gate and allow me and Glory — slowed by exhaustion and bonier than ever — to pass through. The guard is Milar. I can't see him well enough through the lattice to recognize him, but know him by his kindly, gruff voice. Two harvestimes ago we worked together to bring in the grain. A good man and loyal, who could have slid through the gate and run away but made the risky decision to stay.

"Where have you been, Arien, all this time?"

"Visiting," I say, as vaguely as I can. "And dealing with several nasty incidents, both on the way there and on the return journey, which were sent by the gods to try me. But I prevailed." I'm feeling quite proud of myself. "What have you been doing?"

"Sacrificing myself, as Chief Seer told us to." He coughs. "Beware," he says. "This is a one way gate. Those who enter here cannot leave." He's obviously been taught to say these exact words.

"I understand that, Milar."

"You're better off out," he adds. "People are dying all over the place. I sleep at my post so as not to catch the plague from the dwellers below. There is no one wanting to relieve me most days anyway, so it's important I stay. From here I can't smell the sickness, but I watch the big pits being dug to bury the dead, and the fires being lit to throw in clothes, as well as the beds and bedding they died in. But it doesn't seem to do no good."

I still can't see him clearly but hear a loud sigh.

"Please let me in. I have to get back to Chief Seer Yaddair and Neretta."

He hesitates, tells me that it's strange I'm willing to catch the plague just to be with the Chief Seer and First Wife; that it's even stranger that as a baseborn set free by them to go "visiting," I've readily returned to take on the mantle of the lowest of the low again; and that none of the incidents sent by the gods to try me could possibly be even half as dreadful as what's going on in the settlement. Eventually, though, he runs out of reasons for my staying outside the fence, sputters a few times, and gives the beast and me entry. He can't prevent me, as it's only his job to keep dwellers inside the fences. His duties don't include keeping people out, though I assume he can warn them all he wants to. "Don't you go blaming me if you die, Arien," he calls after me.

"I won't be able to," I call back, with an inappropriate giggle. "I'll be dead." I lead Glory to the stables, rub him down, and give him a pail of mash. He twitches both tails in thanks. Reaching up, I tickle him behind the ears before patting him and leaving him to his meal. I have a sudden longing to see Neretta and Yaddair.

Newly grown blooms cluster around the walls of the castrel. They weren't here when I left, have blossomed fast. Flowers tend to be rather dim. These are clearly untouched by the miseries in Vor. They chatter to one another in high boastful voices about the beauty of their petals and the attractiveness of their leaves. It's a competition. One insists that its stigma is by far the loveliest on Lightside. Another counters, saying that hers is finer. "How can you be so vain," I ask, annoyed, "when so many are dying?" Flowers, like Gilan, are notoriously bad listeners. These ignore me, continuing their high-pitched singsong as I knock to be let in.

"What are you doing here?" Neretta's face registers a mixture of confusion and anger as she opens the cookroom door.

"Chief Seer Yaddair said I had to take the children to Gilan's parents. He didn't say I wasn't to come back."

"You know perfectly well what he meant."

"I used his words to guide me, and I don't remember him saying anything that suggested I couldn't return."

In the few short days I've been away Neretta has grown older, with care lines on her forehead and wrinkles around her eyes. Her hair has gone completely grey. Her face has a greenish tinge. Her tunic is ill fitting, looking as though it belongs to a different, bigger woman. While the flowers by the wall have grown tall, she has declined. She stands on the doorstep, half in and half out of the castrel, her basket full of remedies. Its handle is hooked over her arm. She's obviously about to go about her business of tending to the sick. "Don't play word games with me. Why are you here?" she demands again.

The true answer is that I don't know why I'm here. I could be helping Gilan's parents look after the children, playing with the three of them as I often do, or searching for

Radol, if I could only dupe myself into believing that he's still alive. I could be climbing hills and mountains or swimming in safe pools. I could be sitting in the fruit groves beyond the newly erected fences of Vor, well away from Edge, with plenty of windfalls to sustain me, and no chance of dying of plague. I can almost taste the fruit, picture it ripe and warm and myself biting into it, juice dripping onto my tunic. But before I left I had a plan. When I wavered, a voice in my head called me back to the settlement. It was a man's voice, perhaps that of one of the watchers, insisting that I could be of assistance to Neretta and Yaddair without dying. It made me feel special, chosen, filled with new energy, as though I'd be exempt from what the dwellers are forced to endure.

Mother, though, used to say she felt healthiest just before coming down with an ague. Perhaps the dwellers feel at their best just before they succumb; perhaps I'm about to get sick myself. I'm not daunted. Since the episodes in the woods when I bested the murderous trees and wicked boys, and that deadly skirmish with the death dragon on the way back, I imagine myself to be all-powerful, unkillable. I tell Neretta everything I'm thinking. The words tumble out in a rush. Even when I try to bite my tongue I'm unable to curb them.

After plunking the basket down, she manages to wrap her arm around me and shake me at the same time. "You're talking rubbish, as usual. Death dragons indeed! As if you could slay such a monster! More likely it would swallow you for dinner and devour the half-lame steed you rode on for pudding, bathed in its own broth. Where do you get such notions?"

As this is not a question intended for me to answer, I don't, though I do manage a growl or two, which Neretta pays no heed to. That Yaddair would believe me, I have no doubt.

"Take up my basket. How are the children?"

"They're fine." I refrain from telling her that all three of them whine every day to come back to the castrel.

"And how have Gilan's parents received them?"

"Very well." This at least is true.

"The parents are kind? The girls like it there?"

I struggle with my conscience. "Yes," I lie. "They love it."

"Good. That's really all I've been concerned about. As well as your safety, of course."

"I'm fine too."

"You look tired. You've no doubt had a difficult trek-ken, even if you haven't been killing dragons." She snorts with laughter, though her eyes still look tired and grieved. "You've given me a good chuckle today, lifted my spirits. Death dragons, indeed!"

"It was just one, just *one* dragon," I mutter, scratching a piece of dirt off the basket.

"You can tell me everything that really happened as we walk down to the settlement. The old man is already down there, working day and night without a break. Though I wish you'd stayed away, I'm glad to see you," she adds as an afterthought. "And Yaddair will be too. You're a brave girl, even without the dragon's tale, as it were." She pats me twice on the back, just as I patted Glory. We're both loyal beasts, it seems. Neither Neretta nor I mention Gilan.

CHAPTER EIGHTEEN

Milar's description of the settlement was, if anything, less depressing than what I see before me every day. Vor has changed so dramatically it's hardly recognizable. Before the Oscurans came, it was a neat and tidy town, bursting with life and industry. Women rushed to one another's dwellings to chat, cook, and sew quilts. Men and women worked the wolds. Beasts were milked, clothes washed in a safe pool. All that is gone. Everyone is filthy and fearful. Despite Yaddair's rules for the collection of the dead, there aren't many dwellers gathering up and disposing of bodies. Many of the pit diggers appear to have died or fled, clambering over the high fences of Vor or bribing one of the gate guards of the settlement. But a few do come back, thrown out from communities nearby when it's discovered where they're from. Some settlements, I've learned from Yaddair, have set their own sentries around their villages to keep out possible plague carriers from Vor. He has received messages to that effect from the Chief Seer of Braban, along with much-needed supplies. I imagine them shouting news to each other across the pool.

Fires devour the belongings of the dead. Some of the dwellings have burnt down too, but I can't tell whether their destruction was deliberate or accidental. I ask Neretta, but she doesn't answer, her eyes piercing, smudged face grim. An attempt to lock the sick and their relatives in their dwellings is not, for the most part, successful. Many dwellers, weak and ill or searching for food, are wandering in the wolds. The air is smoky and filled with ashes. I choke on it, begin to wear a long piece of cloth tied around my nose and mouth so that I can breathe more easily and my nose isn't always clogged with soot. I like to think also that it protects me from the sick, sets a barrier between them and me. I like to think it, but I don't really believe it. I abandoned my hand coverings long ago. They got in the way and were usually soaking wet, hindering me from my tasks.

The days pass, each day worse than the one before. Sometimes I glimpse the two watchers through the slats of the fence. I can only see parts of their faces because the slats obscure the rest, but it has to be them as no one else in Vor is so tall. I look up at them, feel they're here for me, but am too exhausted to wonder why as I trudge through the unpleasant obligations of my day.

One morning on my way to a sick dwelling, I see them and at the same time hear a voice in my head: *Consider the poisons. Make sure to consider the poisons.* It's the same voice that urged me to come back to Vor. I turn the new words over and over as if I'm looking at the facets of an emerald. They're a key of some sort, but I can't find a way to unlock their meaning. Why would I consider the poisons?

Consider them for what? And what poisons do the watchers mean? I think immediately of toad berries and horn
berries. I consider them, but without a clear understanding
of why I'm doing so. The spiral snakes are also a possibility,
but I'm sure they wouldn't give up their venom without a
fight, and why would I need them to anyway? Can I trust
the watcher who is speaking into my mind? Both of them
are staring at me from the other side of the fence with huge
golden eyes.

"Why do you watch and speak to me?" I ask, thinking
rather than speaking the words.

*Because now your father is gone, you are the only one left
on Kondar who can hear us. The others on Lightside are all
deaf to mind-speak. The art of it is lost.*

This is rather dismaying, although likely true. I've never
met anyone else who has heard the trees or flowers speak, or
can hear dead people, for that matter. I often feel lonely or
afraid because of it. "Who are you?"

*We are The People, curious to see how others live. At pres-
ent we are curious about you.*

A frightening thought occurs to me. They are different
from everyone else. They can speak into my mind. They
appear and disappear at will. They *watch*. "Are you spirits?"

*No. We are people like you, but from elsewhere: from
another planet in this system.*

"So you're not gods either?"

No. We came upon you while journeying.

"So there are other planets?"

*Of course. We are travellers and observers, tasked by our
planet to research the worlds of others, in the solar system and
beyond. But having discovered the sickness in Vor and also*

Oscura, which may soon spread to other communities, we will do our best to help you and your planet recover from its ills.

I've many more questions: Why should I trust them? Are their people all mind-speakers? What is the name of their planet? Why should I consider the poisons? They vanish from the fence before I can ask, leaving me to ponder the strangeness of their words.

Came upon you, they mind-spoke. *While journeying.* Could it be true? Or are they ghosts, ghouls, or gods, in spite of what they whisper to me? I have never seen anyone like them, and am in fact not at all certain that others glimpse them, or surely they would remark on their great height, the paleness of their faces, their golden eyes, and the *thing* I've seen one of them write on without a stylus. If they come from another planet — a planet like the ones Father and Leader spoke of — which is what they are suggesting, do they fly here, as the Oscurans do? They don't appear to have wings.

Walking on slowly, puzzling over what they've said, I wonder if I might ever get responses to my questions. Real life is messy and often frustrating. We may never discover the answers that we seek. At times, perhaps, there are none, unlike in the pat stories that leaders sometimes tell their students to illustrate a point, stories in which there are no loose ends and no unsolved mysteries. Everything finishes tidily, like a well-wrapped parcel tied with yarn. I also wonder whether I might be going mad, as I hear things — the watchers are just one example — that no one else hears. But Father heard the skytrees sing when no one else did — except me, that is. He probably heard much more. Yet Father wasn't mad. At least, no one seemed to think so, apart from Mother occasionally.

I stop to dry my new luggers, which are slippery with sweat, and notice a woman digging a series of small trenches outside her dwelling. "They are for my family," she says sadly. "They are dead, every one of them. They were all I had in the world, and I can't bear for them to be buried in a mass grave. I am weak and ill. Honoured mistress, can you help me bury them? I've heard that you assist where any help is needed."

It's a duty that horrifies me, but how can I refuse? The woman looks close to death herself. We carry her husband and all three of her children out of the dwelling, and lower them into their graves. The little ones look so pitiful I can scarcely keep myself from weeping. They could easily have been Neretta's girls or Miko. It's as if the hard knot in my heart that allows me to function in this drear place has come undone at the sight of them. I feel sick with grief.

There is one pit remaining. "Who's that for?" I ask. "There's no one left in the dwelling."

"It's for me," the woman says simply, lying down in it. She still has her apron on, and pulling it up, hides her face with it. "Cover me with earth, as you did my family."

"I cannot."

"It would be a blessing, as there's no one left to bury me when I die."

"I cannot," I repeat. My job is to try to save life, not extinguish it. Softly, I tell her that.

"I'm sorry you feel you can't, but I understand. It's hard enough to cover the dead without burying the still living, even if they're well on the way to the gods. Thank you for your help."

Her thanks appall me. How can she remain so polite, especially after losing everything she holds dear? I want to yell, scream, kick, curse, am too devastated to respond further to her. "Consider the poisons," I think as I make my way back home, trying to blot her out, incapable of attending to my grisly tasks this day. I shout aloud. Neretta and Yaddair are both at the settlement. My utterance echoes through the empty rooms of the castrel. The message burdens me but I can neither rid myself of it nor solve its riddle. It is only later that I realize the watchers were telling me something about the dying woman's plight, about everyone's plight, about the plague. "Consider the poisons," I repeat more thoughtfully. Maybe I should, though I don't know what was meant. The watchers did say they were trying to help. Anything is possible.

I return to my unpleasant work the next day and the next, but don't see or hear the watchers again. A few days later, deep into the night, I sit bolt upright in my bed. I've finally realized. The watchers were telling me how to cure the plague in Vor as they cure illness by using poison in whichever planet that they live on. They could only pass on the information to me as no one else can mind-speak. Nothing else makes any sense. Why has it taken me so long to realize what they were saying? I might have jeopardized Vor by my lack of understanding. It may well be because I've been sleepwalking through my life lately to ward off dismay at what's happening, but at least now I'm wide awake and have at least part of an answer to one of my questions. In the morning I tell Neretta that I am in need of poison to kill off the pestilence, and that the only two poisons I can think of are toad and horn berries. I don't mention snakes. The memory of their vermillion tangles on the death dragon's back is too painful.

"Load of old rubbish, girl," she says. "The berries would kill off our patients quicker than the plague could."

"Perhaps if we tried just a little, very little, squished up bit of one?" I make a small circle with my thumb and forefinger to demonstrate the amount I'm speaking of.

"The thought is ridiculous. We might as well throw the sick to the spikelfish or thorn eels ..."

"We might as well anyway, for all the good we're doing."

She glares at me. "Stop interrupting. Eat your grain. Bring a pot of water from the safe pool. Put our usual remedies in the basket. Hand it to me so I can be sure you can't sneak any of your poisons into it." She's too critical, too brusque, when she's been so kind of late, but when I think of all she's having to endure I hold my tongue and lower my head. She's not really angry at me, I'm sure. She's angry at the situation, as I am. But then, who wouldn't be?

On our way to the settlement we are wreathed in dismal, frightening, and sinister shade until the sun appears out of the murky haze. It is only visible for a moment, but long enough for me to see that there are shadows under Neretta's eyes and green hollows in her normally plump cheeks. She looks as though all her blood is sitting just below the mantle of her skin. I'm frightened for her.

"Are you feeling quite well?" I ask, my heart rattling in my ears.

"Of course I'm feeling well. Stop asking stupid questions." She is still ready to criticize, but her voice lacks its usual fire. It has become slow, scratchy. Further along the path, quite suddenly, she trips and falls, crumpled as a wrinkled applefruit. She has the Edge-dwellers' plague, I realize now. I kneel down to speak to her. Her eyes stare past me. She doesn't reply. I try to stand her up and drag her back to the castrel, but can't. Her hands have become tightly enmeshed in the lowest needles of an aggressive zigzag tree, which whispers into my brain that it's been on the lookout for just such a victim. It's unyielding, its grip tenacious. As I struggle to free her it shouts that I should let her go. *The woman belongs to me. I have the hunger of a hundred trees, and she is my prey.*

"Shut up and release her or we will cut you down," I yell, enraged. "You are not supposed to be here anyway. It is forbidden. This area was designated by the seers as a safe wood."

The tree hoots derisively and waves its upper boughs. *No one tells me what to do, where to stand, or whom to eat.*

"If you don't let her go we will chop you into little pieces and use you as firewood; we will burn you in a great fire and bury your ashes along with those of the dead." But the tree is either too obstinate to care or too stupid to understand. It attacks even more ferociously, its fierce angular branches filled with needles that pierce Neretta's hands. Spasms of bright green blood erupt from her finger ends. The tree's branches drag her closer, jabbing their needles into her arms and shoulders.

"Don't die, please don't die," I scream, as after another attempt to free her that only leaves her more entangled, I race down to the settlement to find Yaddair. Perhaps we can rescue her from the tree together. But she'll still be sick. And this I know from experience: a few, if well cared for, survive the Edge-dwellers' plague. Those whose blood is green never do. There is something different about them. Thank goodness we sent Yanna and Beklee from Vor.

Yaddair borrows an axe from a dweller he's working with, and we dash up the path. He rapidly separates Neretta from the tree by lopping off its lower branches. I pull her from under them while he takes two furious swipes at its trunk, felling it. It screams as it crashes to the ground that we have killed it, that we don't have the right. The trees around it retreat.

I race to fetch Glory, and we lift Neretta until, belly down so the spines don't injure him, she's lying across his back. Good beast, he carries her carefully back to the castrel. She is very sick, and much weakened by loss of blood. Zigzag needles are still piercing her, sticking out of her shoulders and arms. They resemble the long spines of an orange stabber beast. Because of the needles we can't even cover her without causing her immense pain. They are attached to her by small hooks that have burrowed deeply into her flesh. The sight of all the blood dizzies me, but because it's Neretta I cannot desert her, either by fainting or running away.

"What can we do?" Yaddair sounds desperate. "Our remedies are useless against the pestilence, as we've known since the beginning. And the needles may be an even bigger problem."

"You're right. I wish you weren't, but you are. And I don't think we'll be able to wrest the needles from her unless — until — she's stronger." I have one last thing to try. "Consider the poisons," I murmur.

"What?"

"Never mind. I'll explain later." I rush down the stairs, out of the door and into a forest: not the one we dragged her from, which has clearly been invaded by predators, but one that I know from past visits to be safe as well as reasonably polite.

How are you today, Arien?

"No time to talk, no time at all, busy."

Very well. None of us will bother you then. The speaker tree sounds a little insulted, but not so much as a twig reaches out to touch me, and the other trees don't talk among themselves, though I get the idea they're watching my every move. The flutterers, if flutterers there are, don't sing a single note. I hunt for berries in eerie silence. The toad berries are still unripe, small and hard as pebbles, so I knock a few horn berries into my kerchief with a stick, taking care to evade their thorns and leaves. I daren't put my fingers on any parts of the plant as both Mother and Radol warned me many a time that they're deadly to the touch.

Perhaps you'll find more time for us on your next visit, sulks the speaker tree, his branches drooping.

"I hope so. I really am busy. I'm trying to save a life. Don't take it personally." I run back with the berries, mash one of them with a spoon after boiling it in water, and endeavor to force it down Neretta's throat. Yaddair, bewildered at my actions, tries to wrest the spoon from me. He can't. I hang on to it like the evil zigzag tree hung onto his wife.

Either it is too late to help Neretta or the watchers have been lying. The mixture turns to bright green blood in her mouth and oozes onto her quilt, making an ever-widening stain. It reminds me of when Mother pricked her hand and wiped it on her apron, though this is so much worse. Neretta develops inky boils on her chest. I try to lance them, but they're too dense. She shouts to the gods twice, her voice cracked and harsh. I take her hand, but she wriggles free of me. By late afternoon she is dead. I lean over and close her eyes. It's like losing my mother all over again.

"This is all your fault," Yaddair's eyes are fierce, his irises black. "You have killed First Wife."

"I was doing my best to save her. I loved her dearly." Heartbroken, I stumble up the stairs to my room, collapse onto my side with my legs drawn up, and pull my quilt over my eyes for the first time. There are things much worse than darkness. I know that now. Despite the quilt, I see Neretta's mottled face before me, vow never to try the poison remedy on anyone again.

You will. You will have to. You must find the right one.

"Why don't you just tell me which the right one is?"

Because it differs from planet to planet. You on Kondar don't grow the poison we use on similar illnesses. It might not even be a plant. You must experiment.

"Go away and leave me alone," I cry, "whoever you are."

CHAPTER NINETEEN

I tell Yaddair that I tried the berries as a last resort. Someone — I don't say who — told me that small doses of poison might effect a cure. It doesn't take long for him to apologize. "I'm sorry. I know it wasn't your fault that she died."

"Thank you," I respond quietly. It has been hard enough blaming myself without Yaddair blaming me too. My own feelings of guilt, though, continue to torment me: If only I'd realized sooner that she was sick; if only I'd been strong enough to separate her from the tree myself without wasting time by running for help; if only I'd not fed her the horn berries; if only, if only … but if I'm honest with myself, I know that nothing I could think of, early or late, could have helped her.

"Just like you, Arien, I was distraught. I still am. Just as my stave is my mainstay in the Council House, she was my source of support at home. I didn't praise her nearly enough while she was alive. I took her for granted. Now she's dead" — he chokes over the word — "it's too late to do anything about it."

He ladles water into a cup and drinks a little of it. The cup slips from his hand and shatters. He takes no notice. When I rush to pick up the shards, he stops me. "The whole of Vor is in pieces. A few more won't make any difference."

"We might hurt ourselves if we don't pick up the pieces, Yaddair," I say, using his given name without an honorific for the first time. He doesn't correct me.

"What does it matter? What is a cut when compared to the plague? Dwellers continue to die. There is nothing that Morlova or I can do about it." He collapses onto a chair, his eyes red-rimmed and tears smearing his cheeks. It's frightening to see him weep. He's a man used to winning who is now defeated. I don't know how to comfort him. I've also seen too much death, cannot heal the sick.

"What shall I tell the girls, our daughters? How will I ever be able to explain to them what's happened to their mother?" He jumps up, strides into the backroom, and slams the door before I have a chance to respond. I feel unbearably sad. Bitter too for a moment, as if Neretta died on purpose to spite me. With Yaddair gone, I gather the fragments of pottery. Dagger-sharp, one of them pierces my finger. I feel a curious and unexpected sense of relief as a small stream of orange blood falls to the floor.

Two days later, Yaddair gives me my spade, takes his, and we bury Neretta near the house. My eyes are dry and burning. I cannot cry. We pray at her graveside, leaning on our spade handles, though I have no confidence that our prayers will be heard and know that Yaddair feels as I do. He promises to build a cairn to mark her grave as soon as the plague is over. "We must never forget her," he says as we re-enter the castrel. "She was a good woman."

"I never will. She was my second mother."

"These have been the worst days of my life, but now more than ever I have no regrets about bringing you from Katannya."

"I have no regrets about being here," I reply, to please him. I say nothing about Radol. What is there to say, after all, now that the only place he exists is in my mind?

"I think of you as my oldest daughter, and that will prove a comfort to both of us. We must each be the other's support."

"We will be."

In the afternoon, I ladle gulrid grain into his bowl. I've made a big pot of it so I don't have to think about cooking for a while, but am too grieved to eat any myself. I lay twenty-eight quoinies on the table and sit down opposite him.

"I gave them to you," he says. "They are yours."

"I didn't need to use them so I'm giving them back."

"I will save them for your dowry." He says this with conviction, as if someone will one day want to marry me. I feel somewhat comforted as the tears finally start in my eyes.

We decide that if only for Neretta's sake we must continue our work. "She would hate to think that we have given up trying to heal the sick because of her death," he says. When he pushes his bowl away — leaving much in the bottom of it — I pick up Neretta's basket of remedies, which I've inherited. I slowly fold my long piece of cloth into it. My legs are so heavy I can barely walk. Yaddair fetches his one-eyed stave. "I will stick it in the dirt by the Council House as I no longer feel like a seer. Anyone who wants it can have it."

"You will want it back again soon enough."

"I think not." He hitches his spade over his shoulder. The day is hazy with smoke — fires burn constantly now no matter how sultry the weather — as we make our way down to the settlement to do what we can. Over my tunic I have on an old apron with a jagged tear at the front. Yaddair is in his workman's clothes, his luggers scuffed and filthy, his back bent with age and grief. We look like a couple of dwellers who have laboured too long in the wold. He buries the end of his stave, but it still stands upright, and the eye, wide open, surveys the settlement. I wonder whether Yaddair will ever wear his purple cassock again and reclaim his title, or whether the calamitous events unfolding in Vor have changed him so drastically that he can never again be the luminary he was in the past.

Soot hangs over the dwellings as we leave the settlement, its particles suspended in fog. The dull, sunshineless afternoon is in heavy mourning for Neretta. But above us, in a stand of peach-fruit trees, hundreds of northern twitterers on their way back from the south are tweeting inane feather songs about how slippery wyrms are and how hard it is to catch them. "Stupid little creatures," I rage. "Don't you see what's happening here? Shut your silly beaks and fly away home."

A flood of angry twittering greets my words.

"If you don't shut your beaks, I'll glue them together. Then I'll catch every last one of you, shove you in cages, and eat your eggs for supper," I mind-speak, cutting across their din. That shuts them up at least long enough for us to get out of ear-reach.

CHAPTER TWENTY

Solar came fast. Now, just as fast, it's waning, and the plague wanes too for a while, before surging back. I'm so tired I crawl into bed as soon as I return from the settlement, sometimes not even bothering to wash or eat. It makes little difference how early or late it is. I have to be ready to go back down with Yaddair in early morning, either to help the sick or bring in the harvest, so I sleep whenever I can, though my dreams are peopled — if that's the right word — with evil spirits, spiral and vermilion snakes, death dragons, and three-cornered monsters. Not that I have any idea what a real three-cornered monster looks like, but in my nightmares it resembles an Oscuran with three heads and scissor-blade wings.

One night a member of the dead — a man I sat with until plague claimed him — rises from his grave and tries to catch me. His eyes are red as grunt cheese; his fingers are claws. His face is covered in sores that are the colour of the dirt to which he was consigned. Thump, thump, thump, go his feet, each step sounding like a small explosion as he staggers after me across a burden-beast pasture. I run to the castrel, squeeze my body into the copburde, closing the door after me. The blackness inside is almost as terrifying as the dead man outside. I fear I'll suffocate as I hear his shambling gait on the cookroom floor. A pause. The footsteps start again. Another pause. The steps come closer. I groan in fright. The sound tells him where I'm hiding; he hits the copburde hard: Thump, thump, thump. As his claws curl slowly around the door, I lurch from sleep. I've left my bed, am standing in the hall outside of Gilan's old room, about to fall down the stairs. I grab the banister. The monstrous man has vanished, perhaps into someone else's nightmare, but the racket continues. Somebody is knocking loudly on the cookroom door, I realize. It's a wonder Yaddair hasn't woken.

I dash downstairs, open the door a crack, and peer outside. It's Milar. "What can you possibly mean, Milar, by making such a racket in the middle of the night? You frightened me half to death."

"I'm sorry indeed to disturb you so late, Arien, but there's someone to see you."

"To see *me*? That's not possible."

"It's true. He wanted to see you most particular. He wouldn't take no for an answer, tried to come through the gate though I gave him the most severe warnings about plague, as I've been taught to."

"What does he look like?"

Milar shrugs. "All I can see through the slats is that he's taller than me."

It's a watcher. It must be. Who else could be taller than Milar? Something dreadful must be happening for him to feel the need to come in person now, instead of simply speaking into my mind when I awaken in the morning. I dress hurriedly, though I can't find my luggers. They have to be somewhere, I tell myself, but they appear to be invisible, as my belongings always are when I'm in a panic. I search under bed and table without success, give up and rush out the door in my bare feet. I can hear Milar huffing as he tries to keep up with me.

"I've brought her, stranger," he shouts triumphantly as we approach the gate. "She agreed to come even though the midpoint of night, when spirits fly free to work their magic, is upon us. She stands right here beside me."

Silence from the other side of the fence, followed by something that sounds like a sigh. This cannot be a watcher. "Who is it?" I ask timidly, fearful of the reply.

"Arien ... Arien ... Are you there? Can it really be you?"

"Radol? Is it you? I was sure you were dead."

"My dearest little cousin! I've spent every minute searching for you, have gone from one settlement to another to find you, but was giving up hope; I'd visited everywhere on Lightside except for Vor. I left it until last because it was rumoured that there is an ague here that has killed many and is still thrusting its poisonous claws into the living. I was afraid to arrive here only to find out that you were dead. In the end I dredged up some courage and ran all the way from Dorley — the second-last settlement on my list. It's far away from Vor." He has laced his fingers through gaps in the slats and is clinging to the fence as if for support. His knuckles are white against the dark wood.

"I'm not dead as you can plainly hear. How are you?" I speak quietly, though my heart is pulsing with joy. "The Cauldron erupted, didn't it? We felt it even here."

"It did erupt; I wasn't there, too busy looking for you elsewhere. But I was close enough in Argara to hear the crash and thunder of the explosion. The ground throbbed. Pathways ripped open. Dwellings shattered and vanished beneath the earth. I rushed back to try to find my parents. The whole of Ongis was covered in ash, and streams of lava from underground still divided the landscape. Farther away, some of the rivers of fire had halted but were glimmering red, or hardening into rock."

"And your mother and father? Did you find them?"

"Later I discovered that the Cauldron had given ominous demonstrations of its power before it erupted. Rumblings, shakings, showers of choking ash, and a great deal of smoke jolted the community, all portents of what was to come. Everyone in Ongis took the warning seriously — how could they not? — and ran away. They knew what the Cauldron had done many, many cycles before. No one, as far as I'm aware, was killed, though a few were killed in surrounding settlements such as Argara." He sighs. "My parents moved back to Katannya. I found them there some months later living very close to where we used to live."

I could barely speak. "Thank the gods," I managed to whisper at last.

"Indeed. Let me through the gate." Radol is shaking it almost off its hinges. "I cannot see you properly in the spaces between the boards."

"I can't believe you're here. I thought never to see you again. Are you well?"

"Arien, please stop trying to exchange pleasantries with me and let me in. I can't wait another instant to see you."

"I too wish more than anything to see your face, but once in you must stay here until the plague burns itself out. You might catch it, you might die, and I couldn't bear that. It was bad enough thinking you were dead after the Cauldron exploded."

"You too might catch plague and die, but it didn't stop you from returning voluntarily to aid the settlement. Milar told me of your bravery, of your will to assist the sick, before fetching you."

"Radol, Radol, do you still care for me?"

"Need you even ask?"

"If you do, you will stay on the other side of the fence until the plague is finished and gone. It cannot be long now. We can talk through the slats without your being at risk."

"That's not what I want. I want to be able to see you, stay with you."

"That's not going to happen. Please go away." Reluctantly, I turn to Milar and give him orders not to let Radol in, whatever the rules say. The gateman obeys me because of the tone of my voice, because I've worked so hard with the sick dwellers, and because I'm now accepted as the oldest daughter of Yaddair, thus making me the most important woman in Vor.

I stumble back to the castrel, tears burning my eyes. As I go I hear Radol shouting: "I will knock down the fence or climb over the top of it, barbed though it is, if you don't let me in."

I steel myself not to look back before closing the castrel door, collapsing on my bed with loud painful sobs. The next morning I say nothing to Yaddair, afraid he might undermine my authority and admit Radol.

In the afternoon Radol is still outside the fence, shouting to come in, as he is the day after, and the day after that. Each time I refuse to leave the castrel, instructing Milar to send him away. When Yaddair hears him on the fourth day, I say that the voice comes from a deranged stranger, and Milar is taking care of the problem.

On the fifth day Milar reports that Radol, from what he can see through the slats, appears to be starving, and the young man says he will stay by the fence refusing all food-stuffs until I agree to let him in or he dies, whichever comes first. I gather and prepare a large trencher of neeps, tates, and gulrid grain and hurry to the gate to speak to him.

"You must eat," I say, recalling how he once said the same thing to me. "I will pass food to you. There's a gap at the bottom of the fence just wide enough for a trencher."

"I've made myself perfectly clear. Either you or death will claim me."

My head reels in pity and despair. But I mustn't let his talk sway me the way he clearly means it to. "There's no reason to sound so dire. Think of the fence as if it were Edge. You wouldn't venture across Edge into Oscura, would you?"

"I would if you were there. Arien, you know there is no law to keep me out or you couldn't have been able to return to Vor yourself. I've been searching for you since your parents died and the old seer parted us. I don't aim to lose you just when I've found you again. Please, I beg you, tell Milar to let me in. Or I really will break the gate down."

"Once in, you're trapped. You cannot change your mind. You cannot leave."

"I'm well aware of that. You've already said as much, and Milar has told me too. Often."

"The two of you seem to have had a long conversation." My voice sounds acerbic even to me.

"We've had plenty of time to do so."

I'm desperate to see him again, to be with him from morning till night, to feel his warmth and strength enveloping me. A part of me, though, still wants to insist he stay out of Vor for his own protection, although I also try to convince myself that life is *always* unsafe. If I send him away he could still die — especially if he starves himself — or be killed elsewhere. I know that keeping him out of Vor would be the best alternative, but he's not a child. Ultimately it has to be his decision, not mine. Profoundly conflicted, I vacillate between delight and despair. Finally I make up my mind.

"Eat the food and I'll give you entry," I tell him.

"Give me entry and I'll eat the food," says Radol, who's no fool.

"You won't care for me anymore. I've grown strong as a man. There's nothing in the least pretty about me …"

"I admire strength. I have grown strong also. I had to, if I was to find you. We will be a good match."

"And I'm often cold-hearted from necessity," I continue.

"I will warm you up, never fear."

I can almost feel him grinning on the other side of the fence, but I cling to my earlier decision not to let him in. "You can starve for all I care," I say. "I'm taking the meal I made for you back to the castrel."

In the morning when I go to the fence, he's still there. He screams that there's a three-cornered monster on the hill and it's rushing forward, about to kill him. "Its mouths are open. I can see their fangs. Let me in right now or it'll eat me for sure," he shrieks. "My life is in your hands."

I give up, nodding to Milar to open the gate. It is thundering in the distance, and rain starts to pour down, dousing the three of us as he lets Radol in. I take a quick peek outside before the gate closes. There's no three-cornered monster in sight. "You tricked me!" I yell, losing my balance as I veer around, and careening into mud. Radol howls with laughter, as he and Milar dredge me up.

CHAPTER TWENTY-ONE

Milar has tricked me too. Radol doesn't look starving at all. He has grown even taller and filled out. I'm a little shy of him at first, almost wary. I put out my hand and he grabs it, pulling me to him and hugging me, filthy though I am.

After our initial greetings, he tells me, as he eats yesterday's neeps, that he tried to get back to me the day we were parted, but was stopped, kicked and beaten by guards ordered to keep him away. They dragged him to a deep ditch outside Katannya and left him there, probably expecting him to die. But he was determined to recover. He tells me of the settlements he searched during his trekken to find me; of the fierce battles he had with hostile dwellers, deadly serpents, and the hideous wild beasts of the forests; of his return to Katannya a cycle later to see whether I still lived there, even though it was dangerous to do so. That's when he found his parents. They had been pleading his case. He found my dwelling burned down, with Blanta and Farun inside it. Blanta's burden beast was found safe in her barn, as I'd predicted. Her old dwelling was still standing, an emblem of evil times.

They deserved to die, I think viciously. Farun murdered my parents, and Blanta received the proceeds in the form of a home much better than her own, together with my family's fields. But I hate to think that the dwelling I grew up in is gone. "What happened to the beast?" I ask Radol.

"I asked my parents and the dwellers who lived around the house. People I knew whom you'd no doubt know too. Apparently the beast had been given to another runaway family from Ongis, along with a bag of grain that was found. The family was close to starving. The Chief Seer declared that Blanta's old dwelling was at their disposal."

"A good ending to a bad story," I say unsteadily.

"A good ending indeed. The old seer told me that Blanta's original dwelling is yours if you want it. He'll find somewhere else for the family living in it now, or you can collect rents from them. He realized, after the discovery of the burden beast and the entreaties of my parents, that he had done both you and me an injustice."

"I'm glad of that, but I don't want Blanta's dwelling. I don't want to collect rents from dwellers who can't afford to pay them. I want never to go back to Katannya even if your parents *are* there. Bad memories of the place haunt me."

"I thought you'd say that. You may, of course, live wherever you like, as long as I can live with you. Strong as a man you may be, with arms like the weighty boughs of skytrees, but I will still and always be your protector." He smiles.

"I will protect you too," I say earnestly. "I promise." It is my turn to speak of what's happened since we parted.

I tell him of my life in Vor, my first cycle there as a base-born, bereft and lonely; the family's acceptance of me; the poison forests, death dragons, vermilion snakes, and the heart-breaking death of Neretta; my informal adoption by Yaddair. We are each astonished by the other's story, hold hands across the table as we commiserate before discussing what we need to accomplish to make the future happier. Radol says that if I'm willing, we will always be together, which pleases me immensely. He then says we could make a home of our own here if I wish to after the plague is over, and I grow somber.

"Who knows if it will ever be over? Perhaps our lives will end before that happens."

"They won't," he says firmly, and I pray that he's right. We go to sleep early. I put him into Gilan's old room, as it is so close to mine. I hate to be parted from him.

He and Yaddair meet in the morning. "You may stay here," says Yaddair, who is initially somewhat surprised to find a tall young man in the cookroom, eating a bowl of gulrid grain and powdered freeps that I've made him. "I'll be glad to have more company — and more help. But you won't stay in Arien's room, you'll stay in Second Wife Gilan's next door, which I hope is where you slept last night."

"I did, sir."

"Until you're wed, that is. I suppose that's your intention."

"It is." Radol grins. I feel myself blushing.

"I can't say I blame you, though she can be even more stubborn than my late wife when she wants to be. That said, I'll be lonely without her if the two of you leave."

"You'll get your daughters back," I interrupt. "You'll be too busy running after them to miss me at all."

"That's as maybe. Enjoy the flounces on Gilan's couch and the wall-hangings," he says, turning back to Radol and winking.

Radol bows. "Anywhere to lay my head is fine. I've become used to sleeping on stony ground, on ice, and in ditches."

"You can remain next door to Arien. No nearer, mind. No creeping around while I'm asleep."

"As if I would." Radol grins again. "Thank you, Chief Seer."

"Please call me Yaddair, as Arien does. I don't need the title, and I don't deserve it. At the moment I feel I'm Chief Seer of nowhere and nothing." He is still bent over, crook-spined, like an ancient dweller.

Old man, you talk such rubbish, Neretta remarks in my head. I can't help but agree.

CHAPTER TWENTY-TWO

Pouring from the skies without cease, the rain is a sullen precursor to Icer. The pathways flood so there's no way I can get down to the settlement, which I selfishly think of as a blessing; it means that Radol can't put his health at risk by accompanying me. The weather doesn't improve; rain is still pelting down in torrential bursts when three Oscurans swoop down from the sky and dissolve in the wold. It happens just as Radol and I are fetching pots of water from the new rain barrels before they overflow, spilling the precious liquid.

The Oscurans leave a blackish smear on the grass. *Help us, help us. We are dying,* come the disembodied voices. I tremble, but the smear — all that is left of them — is soon washed away, so thankfully there's no need to bury them. We hasten back to the castrel, water swishing out of our pots. Some of the scissor-winged monsters must still be alive in Oscura, then. I've been hoping that the plague killed them all off, for we've seen nothing of them since Farlis. It is disgraceful of me, I know, to wish for the death of any creature, but I can't help it. They may not be evil in themselves, but they visit evil upon us.

I'm grateful that the people of Vor didn't see them, as luckily — if anything of the sort can be called luck — the Edge dwellers fell close to the side of the castrel that faces away from the settlement. There would be chaos and terror otherwise, and there is enough of that already. As it is, Radol is greatly alarmed — for my sake, he says. He's never seen such creatures before though I've spoken of them since he came. I too am alarmed. I never thought to see them back. I denied the possibility to myself so I could continue doing what I'm doing without fear of seeing them crash into the ground, spreading more contagion. I was hoping the plague would burn itself out.

The rain ceases at last, wind blowing black clouds towards Edge. Thankfully, no more Oscurans arrow-dive into the wold. There is no longer anything to keep me at the castrel during the day, though I linger as long as I can. I know I must return to the settlement to try to ease the pains of the sick, but I don't want Radol beside me as I work and tell him so as firmly as I can. Through almost daily exposure, I believe I've built up some kind of immunity, something I call "an ague exemption"; he is freshly exposed to contagion, so I fear greatly for him. But just as I was once Neretta's assistant, he insists on becoming mine. He appears beside me on the path, laughs at my warnings, and begins to spend his days as I do, wiping cool cloths over fevered bodies and giving remedies that in nine cases out of ten are useless. When Yaddair needs him, he doesn't hesitate, but helps collect the dead and dig graves in which to bury them. He doesn't show a trace of fear. I am desperately worried about him, but Yaddair is pleased. "He will make a fine husband for you," he says, after watching Radol shovelling out dirt to make a new trench.

"If he lives," I say to myself.

But despite the constant risk of infection, Radol doesn't become sick. If anything he appears stronger and more courageous as each day passes. There is a dangerous glint in his eye, as if he could take on the ghastly death dragons and chop off their heads with a single swing of the axe. So I stop picturing him in a grave, just as I have long since stopped imagining myself in one. Occasionally, though, I see in my mind's eye the wretched woman who buried her dead husband and children before climbing into a grave herself, and I shiver.

One early morning as I awaken the sun spills into my eyes like boiling water. When I try to get out of bed, my legs collapse under me. At first I think I might have a crawler bite. I saw the web of one recently, hanging from my ceiling, too high to knock down. Crawler bites can be nasty though they're not usually lethal. I ache intensely but don't feel the itchy stinging of a bite anywhere on my body. I uncover my arms to try to look for one and it is then, half-blinded by my scalded eyes, I detect the telltale blue boils on my wrist. They are probably all over my body if the pain I feel, rapidly becoming excruciating, is anything to judge by.

I hold my hand up to examine the rash more closely. My forearm shakes violently. The spasm that shoots like a firebolt from my fingertips to the crown of my head is so agonizing I scream. Yaddair and Radol come running. The pestilence has caught them, as well as me, unawares. Radol doesn't recoil, as I feared he might, but rushes to my bedside;

Yaddair appears to be praying to Vor's non-existent gods. Neither speaks to me. They are too busy working on my body. I'm too sick to feel embarrassed as they strip my tunic off to examine me. Radol finds his name engraved in green on my arm and wipes his eyes. He runs to fetch the medicine basket and both he and Yaddair make little shushing sounds as they tend to my boils.

"Stop that nonsense," I whisper hoarsely. "Those remedies never do any good. Take away the janny and the maymint. The nettlers too. They're worse than useless." My lips are parched and cracking, but I know water won't help. When it's offered, I push it away.

"I refuse to stand idly by and watch you die," says Radol.

"Sit then." I laugh hoarsely.

"Be serious."

"There is nothing else to do, unless ... unless ..." Mired in a fog of confusion, I forget what it is I want to say.

"Unless what?" asks Yaddair, his voice impatient.

I can't remember, try to jolt my mind into action. Like an ancient burden beast lying in the middle of the path, it resists.

"I ... need ... poison ... berries ... mash ... one," I utter at last.

"What kind? A horn berry?"

I can't tell who's speaking. My eyes are now so sticky they're welded shut. "No!" I whisper. "No!" A horn berry killed Neretta. Or at least, it didn't cure her. It amounts to the same thing. I haven't dared try a poison remedy on anyone since. But now I've become sick, I can test it on myself. I don't hold out much hope, but know it's my only chance. "Toad ... berries — ripe now." If they had only been ripe earlier, I would have dosed Neretta with them.

"They will kill you, stupid child."

"I … have the blue boils…. They're festering. The plague … holds me fast in its grip. I'm dying …" The ghosts of other dead — those I've attempted to help — float across my mind as if inviting me to go with them. The prospect is almost tempting. It would mean an end to pain.

Yaddair shakes his head. "Your experiments didn't help First Wife," he responds. "They won't help you. I forbid any more of them."

"I must have them … now. Get them … now."

"Yaddair, we must do what Arien asks. It is the only possible way to save her. And if we don't listen, and she succumbs, how will we feel then?"

"Help me, help me quickly, I'm dying." I mind-speak the words, but no one answers.

"I tell you, the berries will only kill her faster. I don't want to see her die as Neretta did. There must be another way."

"If there is, neither Arien nor I have found it, though together we've treated at least thirty dwellers. And she treated many more when working with your wife. This is her only chance." Radol breaks off, shouting, "This is what she wants. This is what I want. Forget the discussion. It gets us nowhere." He rushes out of the castrel in search of berries.

I pray silently to the watchers and to the gods that I suddenly believe in for him to return safely from the deadly forests in which toad berries grow. Unable to speak any longer, I hear Yaddair pacing as I fall asleep. I wake from a dream of my dwelling burning down in Katannya when I hear Radol's footsteps on the stairs. He carries the berries to my bedside, touching my arm and telling me he has them in a cloth. He mashes one and tells me he has done so. Yaddair, who has given up objecting, feeds the berry to me. It tastes vile, like malherbs mixed with bitterfruit, chokechurls, and ashes. I swallow hard, manage not to vomit, and fall back to sleep.

Evening divides into intervals of sleeping and waking. I'm not sure which is which. Much later, perhaps morning, when I wake for about the fifth time, I wonder whether I'm still alive. Until my eyes come unstuck, I'm unsure of where I am and whether I'm really awake or experiencing the dreams of the dead. Meanwhile Radol forces another berry into me, and my mind drifts until I see visions of fire-tipped mounts and lush red-mauve forests under verdant skies. Whenever I manage to open an eye, Radol and Yaddair are sitting on either side of me. I try to keep in mind what Yaddair once said: that I will have a long life. The berries don't kill me, but they don't seem to be helping much either.

"Vermilion snakes," I croak. "Near the death dragon I killed."

Yaddair sketches a route that leads from the castrel to Gilan's dwelling. "It must be somewhere along there," he cries. "Find a strong bag to hold them in and go."

"Careful," I croak. "Careful, careful. Take Glory the swift beast. He will know where to find them."

Radol rushes out, risking his life for me. He returns hours later with a bag of writhing snakes, declining to tell Yaddair and me what kind of horror he and Glory had to endure to retrieve them. That's fine. I'd rather not hear. If I were healthier I'd be throwing up at the thought of the crimson slithering serpents, which almost cost me my life. Now they may save it.

"We must take one out," says Yaddair. "Hold it by the head on both sides of it jaws so it can't bite us, and squeeze

its venom into a bowl immediately. Take care." I drop off
to sleep. When I wake Radol is holding my mouth open as
Yaddair drops a bead of venom onto my tongue. My gorge
rises, but I manage to swallow it and keep it down.

The next day, I'm thrilled to find I can see again, even
if blurrily, through one eye. I pray that the worst is past.
Desperate with thirst, I demand water. Following discussion
with Yaddair, as well as Morlova — who has come to see
how I am and give me his blessing after hearing rumours of
my sickness — Radol spoons a tiny amount into my mouth.
Mercifully, it doesn't turn to blood. I still have a raging thirst
so he feeds me another spoonful. I fall into a deep sleep and
am oblivious to anything that happens during the afternoon
and evening. I wake deep into the night and drink more
water. Yaddair is sitting next to me. "I am tempted to believe
in the gods again," he whispers in my ear. "This is nothing
less than a miracle."

"Don't be silly," I whisper back hoarsely. "If you insist on
believing in anything, it should be slithery snakes in vermilion skins."

On the third day, starving, I ask Yaddair for steamed
tates. He's never cooked before and keeps asking me how-to
questions, until I grow annoyed and tell him to just get on
with it before I expire from hunger.

"No fancy cooking, then?"

"Don't be silly. Just put the tates in water and boil them
in a pot over the fire. You do know what a pot is, don't you?"

In the end he does a good job, donning one of Neretta's
flowery aprons from the copburde and parading around in
it while I eat the small amount he's cooked. I can't help but
smile, though my face feels stiff and dry. After I beg for more

food, he refills my bowl in the cookroom and twirls into my room with it like a dancer. I laugh out loud. This is a Yaddair that I've never encountered before, relaxed and humorous. He bows when presenting the bowl. I bolt down the mashed tates as if I'm a puppy-drog. It makes my belly hurt, as does my laughter, but heavy with food I feel light in spirit.

Radol feeds me another drop of snake venom. The next day I notice my boils are beginning to recede, leaving bluish marks like thumbprints in their wake. I quit my bed, not for the grave, as I'm sure everyone, including myself, recently expected, but a chair in the hallway. "I'm cured, or at least, well on the path to it. How strange that a poisonous snake could mend what's ailing in the settlement," I remark in wonderment.

"Strange indeed. But you're right. What is working for you will likely cure others too." Radol looks ecstatic.

Yaddair agrees. "This remedy might well cure all the sick. I will send out an order to the dwellers to hunt carefully for vermilion snakes before Icer overtakes us and the snakes die, or hibernate in hidden places." Slowly, he begins to straighten his spine until he stands erect and tall, resembling his old self. He has the air and assurance of a Chief Seer of Vor once again; I can see by his bearing that he at last feels useful in our ongoing battle against the plague. I feel the same way myself. Finally, we're winning!

At my request, when Radol goes out to minister to the sick and provide them with a remedy, he also searches for the stave. He discovered it, as he tells me later, planted in dirt outside the Council Chambers, its eye shut as if asleep. It had been growing, had small tangled roots visible after Radol pulled it out. "It's astonishing, when you think about it," he says, "that no one picked it up."

"That's because you've never seen the dwellers' reaction to it. They're afraid of what they consider to be its magical properties."

"Really? It's just a grimy old stick. I suppose Yaddair could crack someone over the head with it, but it doesn't seem like his style."

"The eye opens wide and glares at people. It's as if it can see their secret wrongdoings. Even I found it a bit frightening at first."

"Ha," replies Radol. "You? You're perfect. You can't possibly have done anything wrong."

"That's what *you* think."

We laugh uproariously, later returning the stave to its rightful owner. Yaddair touches the hidden lever and the eye snaps open, before spinning round and round. Radol jumps back in fright.

"Still working!" shouts Yaddair, grinning like a mischievous child. I see the cheer on his countenance, and the comical grimace on Radol's, as he realizes he has been taken in by a piece of wood. I rejoice that these men, whose faces were recently bathed in gloom, are now so mirthful. I welcome the thought that the future, which only a handful of days ago looked so closed, so bleak, is now sprung open with possibility.

CHAPTER TWENTY-THREE

The last victim of the Edge-dwellers' plague is lowered, not into a public pit like many others, but a private burial place, as there is once again time to carry out the traditional rites of death. All who remain alive in Vor gather around, each throwing a handful of earth and grass, as is the custom, into the grave of the deceased, a girl who — as the dwellers remark — had become so distant from Vor in her trekken to the gods that she was unable to turn back, even after receiving three doses of the remedy.

"Why you throwing earth in there?" asks a small boy.

"So the dead cannot rise again," says the woman holding him.

"Why you throwing grass in there?"

"It holds the promise of new life," says Yaddair.

I tremble at their words, because unlike the others I can hear the girl accusing me from beneath the ground, moaning that it *could have*, *should have* been me. If it were not for the watchers, I tell her, it *would have* been me. But she is too far gone to listen. I stand by her grave as snow begins to stipple the dirt, gathering speed and heft in the sudden and unexpected onset of Icer.

"Thank you, Watchers, for the gift of my life," I mind-say. I half expect a response, but there is only the dead girl's pitiful voice, like the sad song of a far-off twitterer, lapsing finally into silence as the snow falls quick and soft about our gathering. Perhaps, like Kondar's gods, the watchers have gone away.

In time Vor begins to resemble itself again, with the exception of the funereal cairns that cover the dead, which are everywhere. The settlement recovers, the market brings in new foodstuffs, and pathways are thronged with people again instead of corpses. Parents who have lost their children agree to take children who have lost their parents into their dwellings and make them their own. While this is happening, Yaddair goes on a trekken to fetch his own children, Yanna and Beklee, and tell them the sad news about Neretta. He takes two of our new puppy-drogs with him to distract them. He comes back with not two children but three, surprising me. "Gilan doesn't love Miko. She is incapable of love, too busy looking after herself. And his grandparents are too old to care for him on a regular basis. They still believe he's my child, as no one has ever told them otherwise. Perhaps it's best that they never know the truth."

"Perhaps it is. They might throw Gilan out, and then she'd be knocking on our — your — door again." I make a wry face.

"It's your door too. I've promised to take him back to them at least once a cycle, so they can see him grow up."

"You're a kind man, Yaddair."

"Not kind. Selfish. Although I've always wanted one, I've never had a son. Miko will fill the void very well," he says, watching as the child tries to help the dwellers take down the fence, but ends up smashing a miniature hammer — Milar's gift to him — on someone's toe. "Besides, he loves Beklee and Yanna madly, he copies their every move. They call him 'little brother.'"

As I go to relieve Miko of his hammer, I'm reminded of my childhood with Radol, how he protected me then, and how he tries to protect me now. A youth no longer, he's become a strong, caring man.

Chapter Twenty-Four

Walking away from the settlement one snowy day after visiting a former patient — one who, like me, owes her life to the vermilion snakes — I see something I hoped never to see again.

The clouds shift and darken as if a storm's coming, and I look up, as Neretta once did. Several pitch-black creatures are flying across Vor. At first I think them flutterers, giant valkons perhaps, on their way south. But as they change direction and arc like spears into the snow, I know them for what they are: Edge dwellers of Oscura.

I am not the only one to see them. As they plummet, young boys emerge from their dwellings. No longer afraid of the plague, they streak like swift beasts across the snow to the fallen Oscurans, whom they proceed to taunt and kick as the creatures shatter into filmy pieces.

No, no, no. It hurts, it hurts. Stop, stop.

"Leave them alone," I cry. But it's too late. They're all dead.

"They were dying anyway," snivels a grunt-faced boy.

"That's no excuse for violence." I'm surprised at the anger raging inside me and try to quell it. "It really isn't," I say more gently. "They didn't mean to visit plague on us."

"So what? We were just having a bit of fun," he says. "I'd rather slide down the hill but I don't have a sledge."

"You're Milar's relative, aren't you? I've seen you with him at harvestime."

"Yes, Milar's my father's brother. What's it to you?"

Despite his hostility, I manage to remain calm. "Perhaps he can teach you how to make a sledge if you ask him politely. Milar's good at making things out of wood. There's plenty of it since the fences were knocked down. You're welcome to take whatever supplies you need."

"Thanks," he says sarcastically, as the other boys look on.

I understand how he feels. Who, after all, am I to cast blame? I've wished the creatures dead and gone from Kondar many times. I've said they were no better than grinders and likened them to fiends and death dragons. I've gloated over their deaths, dreamed of taking Yaddair's axe to them, hacking off their wings and in one nightmare their heads. Now we have the cure to the plague, I'm no longer frightened, though I still shudder at the sight of them. But unlike Milar's nephew, I've come to realize that I don't need or even want revenge. They're probably no more evil than we are. We actually have much in common: We're all dwellers of Kondar, terrified of a fatal disease, trying to escape its clutches. "Bury them if there's anything left to bury, and we'll say no more about it."

"I lost my mother, you know," he shouts, as I resume my climb to the castrel. "I lost her and I'll never see her again. Those monsters gave her the plague."

CHAPTER TWENTY-FIVE

We are sitting in the cookroom talking after our noon meal, trenchers and spoons still on the table. Yaddair is down at the settlement, and the children are outside playing. I can hear Miko's throaty chuckle. Radol moves around the table to sit next to me. Taking my hand, he says without preamble that it's time to get married. "There's no reason we should wait any longer," he says. "You're eighteen cycles now …"

"Almost," I interrupt.

"And it's something we discuss nearly every day. You said, 'After the plague,' and that's exactly where we are now, thank the gods. I want to marry you. The plague is over."

I start to fidget. "Not really."

"How can you say that? There've been no signs of it for many, many days, almost a whole season. Your remedy worked on everyone."

"The Edge dwellers are still affected by it. Three or four of them dived into the snow close to the settlement today."

"What have they to do with us? Their sickness cannot harm us any longer."

"But they're still suffering. We're from the same planet and therefore, like it or not, our lives are intertwined with theirs. Radol," I say, making a sudden decision about something I've been considering for a long while, "I'm going to Oscura. Will you come with me?"

He drops my hand, picks up a spoon, twists its stem, and bangs it back on the table. "You're out of your mind."

"Probably. I've been wondering lately whether I am. But that's irrelevant to what I want to do in Oscura. I've decided to go so I'm going. You must decide for yourself whether you'll come with."

"Not too long ago I said I'd go anywhere to be with you, even Oscura. I wasn't lying, though I never expected it would happen," he says gruffly. "But it's happening now, so I must accompany you." He's still occupied with the spoon, whirling it round and round like a child's spinning top. Every time it falls over he picks it up and spins it again. He avoids my gaze.

"So despite giving that spoon a good twirling you wish to cross Edge with me?"

"It's not that I wish to, because I don't. It's perilous. It may kill both of us. No one, to my knowledge has ever been there and if anyone has, he certainly hasn't returned to tell his tale. I want us to stay safe in the castrel and help Yaddair care for the children, hopefully have our own. I want you to become the first female seer, as Yaddair suggested just yesterday. I want to farm the wolds, digging my spade into its rich loam. I want us to enjoy a normal life, able to go where we wish, free from fears about plague."

"Then you should stay here."

"No, I can't. I have to go with you because whatever you want to do must be really important or you wouldn't be doing it." He pauses. "I also have to go with because my life would be empty without you. But no matter how hard I try to protect you, it's likely that neither of us will ever return."

"We probably won't," I agree.

"But I will go with you if you promise never to leave me, no matter how long or short our lives may be."

"I shall never leave you. If you leave *me*, I will follow you, even if you travel to places where there are huge, slimy snakes slithering across the wold and coiling around dwellings in their hunt for short, dark-haired victims with strong arms." I grin.

"That's all I needed you to say." His lips start to curve upward, stop just short of a smile.

CHAPTER TWENTY-SIX

Five days later, in the middle of the night — we waited for Yaddair to go to his room before secretly preparing for the glacial, dark place that's our destination — we're ready to embark on our wildly dangerous task. I've told Radol why we're going. We're wearing all the clothes we can muster. I can't tell what Radol has on beneath his cloak, but his girth is doubled. The hood he's wearing hides his eyes so I can't speculate about what he's thinking, though I would be surprised if he's entertaining pleasant thoughts. I still feel that he's loath to go, hates the thought of it, and is doing it entirely for my sake.

I must look ridiculous. "Don't laugh at me," I warn.

"I would never do that," he replies, as he draws back his hood for a moment. With a twinkle in his eye, he surveys my outfit. I have on two nightgowns, a tunic, an apron, leggings, two pairs of stocklets, my scarf, my luggers, and a wool-beast cape. I'm also wearing my old hand warmers, which are stiff and cracked, and a purple seers' skullcap I took from a peg in the cookroom. It is perched on my head like a flutterer. I lost my own hat in the settlement when it rolled away in a squall.

"No, I would never do that," he repeats, choking back laughter as he pulls his hood forward again.

"Stop it. This is serious work we're about to do." But in truth, I'm glad of his foolishness. It's a release. "You don't look too elegant yourself," I note. I wind my scarf around my neck, and we commence our trekken across the wold. Radol leads the way. Although it's Icer, I'm sweating like a grunt. We each have a lit torch, and I've attached a large pouch to my belt. What's in it isn't money, but the promise of life. I can feel it bumping against my thigh.

As we advance towards Edge, it grows colder and greyer. The torches throw halos of fire into the dimness. To my surprise, I see one of the watchers. He's so close that he's standing within my torch's arc of light as Radol forges ahead. *Those who hear and see what others cannot, may easily become bewitched by Oscura. Go and return fast, Arien. Do not get tangled in Oscura's spells.*

I have no idea what the watcher means about bewitchment, but I blink and he disappears before I can ask him. Lightning flashes. My sweat turns to ice. I catch up with Radol and clutch his free hand. We slow our pace, but now Edge seems to be advancing towards *us*, not slowly, as once noted by Father, but in a fierce assault of cold and darkness. A monstrous gale rushes by, extinguishing the torches. In an instant we are caught up in swirling, stinking black fog. Although my eyes are open I can see nothing at all, not even Radol. I scream.

"Hold on," he shouts. "Don't let go of my hand or we may never find each other again. Just keep walking. If you do what I say, we'll be fine." We move forward blindly, buffeted by the gale, through more dizzying displays of lightning. I see high mountains belching smoke and flames, and patches of green sky before we're pitched back into blackness. Thunder crashes around us.

As suddenly as it captured us, Edge lets us go. We are standing in a clearing on a shining pathway of frost. Above us shine two bright crescents and what appears to be a dim replica of the sun. These must be the moons of Kondar. Leader was wrong when he said with such assurance that there were only two. There are also a hundred million pinholes in the sky, through which glittering shards of ice burn bright and sharp, like shimmering eyes. They must be the stars. Their chill pierces my bones, but I can't look away. I need to stay here and count every one of them. I cannot return to Lightside until I do. Perhaps there are gods after all. If so, these must be them. I now understand what the watcher meant. I'm entranced. I always imagined Oscura as a frightening dismal place, but I was completely wrong. It flashes with light and colour.

"Come on," says Radol, pulling me by my scarf. "We didn't come here to gawp. We must do what we have to and get out of here, or we'll freeze to death."

Unlike Radol, I have no desire to move. I want to stand and gaze at the brilliant heavens forever, but he won't allow it. I'm itching to punch him. The idiot feels he's protecting me as he drags me along the path as if I'm a milk beast. Although I slip and slide, I continue to look up until an Oscuran flies in front of the glistening eyes in the sky. It swoops down and lands in front of us, folding its wings. It has a surprisingly friendly face, with dark features much like my own. It doesn't at all stink of fish. That must have been the Oscurans' dying smell. And it's not in black rags, but is many hued, translucent, its skin shaded purple and red and orange, like a colourful twitterer.

"Can you hear me?" I mind-speak.

Yes. I am the guardian of the night. Who are you?

"We are Lightsiders."

I always thought they existed. But the sick ones who cross Edge in search of a cure for their illness do not return, so I never knew for certain. What do you want here?

"Get on with it," growls Radol, who can't hear a word of the conversation the Oscuran and I are having. "Drop the bag and let's get out of here. I don't intend to die waiting for you. The Edge dweller looks terrifying, and as I said earlier, we must leave before we freeze. You know that to be true. I am half-frozen already, and you must be too." Oscura has turned him into a coward determined to leave at any cost, just as it convinces me that I need to stay. I pray to the smokies of Edge. I pray to their gods to allow me to remain. I know I could do so much good.

"Your sick ones died," I mind-speak to the Oscuran when my prayers are done. "But it was through no fault of the Lightsiders."

We die here too.

"I understand. I have come here to help you, just as others helped me."

You cannot help us. We are all dying. Soon there will be none of us left.

This, I remember, is what I once wished for, but I don't desire it any longer. I remove the pouch from under my cape awkwardly because of the hand warmers I'm wearing, and set it onto the ice. "Consider the poisons," I mind-speak. "Make sure to consider the poisons. But don't open the pouch until you're ready to use the remedy: snake venom." I explain to the guardian of the night how to extract it. The snakes have not been killed by cold. I can see them writhing inside their fabric prison. "If this doesn't work, another noxious substance will."

I am grateful for having had this chance. My mind is in perfect sympathy with the universe. I feel at one with the creature and reach towards it in a dreamy gesture of friendship. It is still questioning me about the poisons, but I can't respond, as Radol spins me around, yelling that we must leave *right now*. I ignore him. He shoves me violently on the shoulder before wrapping one hand like a vice around my wrist, wrenching me away from the Oscuran and almost tearing my arm off in the process. "We have to get out of here," he bellows. "Move!" As if I, whose hearing is so acute I can hear the whispered songs of skytrees, can't hear him.

"No, no, I'm not ready to go yet!" I shriek. "The gods are with me. I will never leave." I kick him hard on the knee. He groans and releases my hand.

"I have to get you out of here. Either you help or I drag you." He is still shouting. He throws his hood back so I can see his ugly wild-drog face, narrowed eyes. He pushes me again, hard. His fingers dig like talons into my shoulder.

How could I ever have thought I cared for him? He's a vicious brute who only cares for himself, for his own comfort. He's a bit *chilly* so we must *leave*. I despise him, violent as he is and blind to the miraculous beauty of Oscura, to my desperate need to remain and contemplate its wonders, pray to its gods. But abhor him though I do, I have no choice but to stumble up the frosty path in front of him. "Let me be, Radol. I need to stay. You go back without me."

"No. Either we go back together, or we die here. And I don't want to die here. You're not going to either." He gives me another shove. Even if he's much bigger and stronger than I am, and can keep me moving up the glassy slope, he can't silence my insults, or stop me from being captivated by the millions of icy stars aglow in the heavens. I trip over my feet and fall as I gaze upward. He pulls me up and keeps me moving with a series of threats and jabs to my back.

"I hate you. You're a disgusting beast. Let me go. I want to stay here forever and gaze at the sky."

"Get up the path. We're going home, back to Vor, whether you want to or not. If you don't move faster, I'll pick you up and carry you." He says nothing further, but forces me to approach Edge, bully that he is. As we close in on it, the stars suddenly vanish behind a dense veil of gloomy fog, crashing us into darkness. Their witchy hold over me disappears in an instant. The gods were imaginary. My legs give way, but I manage to stop myself from falling a second time, from plunging into the void.

I realize with a shiver how freezing I am. My nose and feet are so numb they don't seem to belong to me. My hands burn with cold; frost has bitten both my ears. I stare at Radol, and as my eyes become accustomed to the dark I see the frozen tears on his cheeks. How could I ever, ever, have thought him hateful?

"I'm so sorry," he says. He sounds abject. "I don't usually go around pushing people. But I couldn't think of any other way to free you from Oscura's spell."

"That's exactly what it was: a spell. If you hadn't done what you did, I would have frozen to death, just as the Edge dwellers burned in the sun of Vor. The smokies dropping fire on snow, the silent gods, the brilliant star eyes, the guardian of the night — I was enthralled by all of them. I'd completed my task but wanted to remain, to become an Oscuran. I would never have made it out of Darkside if I'd been alone, Radol. I would have perished on the ice. I owe you my life."

We are speaking to each other in the bleak penumbra of Edge. We still have to trekken through it. Radol draws me to him and kisses me once on the forehead and twice on the cheeks. His kisses are light as a gauzefly's wing. I feel as though I'm enfolded in a warm quilt, as if I'll never feel cold again. He used his strength *for* rather than *against* me, I realize now. For my sake, he battled the illusions of Oscura, and he won. I'll never forget it. Although I've been terrified of Edge for as long as I can remember, I'm now eager to reach out to it, to travel once more with him through its black and deathly portals, to experience the worst that darkness has to offer. I am not in the least afraid, for it is the final obstacle — slight as it now seems — that stands between me and my life with him, the very last test we must undergo on our journey back to the light, where Yaddair and the children will be waiting for us.

Acknowledgements

Many thanks to my husband Michael and my son Adam who helped out and were exceedingly patient. Both made valuable suggestions and assisted me in editing the book.

To the rest of my supportive family, including Jamie, my lovely daughter.

To my supercalifragilistic agent, Margaret Hart, who performs miracles on my behalf.

To former Dundurn editor Michael Carroll and the staff at Dundurn for accepting *The Plagues of Kondar*.

To Kirk Howard and Diane Young of Dundurn, who brought my novel to fruition and published it.

To my kind editors, Cheryl Hawley and Jennifer McKnight, who were quick to pick up on my errors.

And to all my friends, writerly, neighbourly, and Shakespearean!